D0822775

Edge of the Heat 2

by Lisa Ladew

All characters appearing in this work are fictitious. Any resemblance to real persons or organizations, living or dead, is purely coincidental.

Copyright © 2014 Lisa Ladew

Chapter 1

Think Emma, think! Calm down and breathe.

Emma forced herself to take a second to relax and formulate a plan. She was still holding on to the bathroom door, eyes frantically darting around the small Westwood General hospital room to be sure Norman wasn't going to jump out at her from some hiding place. Which was silly, there *were* no hiding places in this tiny room. Still, she was learning it was better to be safe than sorry with her ex-husband, who she knew was a dirty cop, but who also just might be a sociopath.

Norman was probably the one who had bugged her house. He for sure was the one who chased off every man she had tried to date over the last several years. She was starting to suspect he was really the one who told Reece she 'liked it rough', prompting the scumbag doctor to try to rape her but pretend she really wanted it that way. And if the horrible feeling she got when he had mockingly said "Who is going to throw me out, your boyfriend?" was correct, he may have done something horrible to Craig. She couldn't be her usual naive and rose-colored glasses self anymore. Her eyes were open now, at least when it came to Norman.

She took some deep breaths and tried to think what she should do first.

Call Craig.

Yes, call him first. Maybe she would get lucky.

She felt her pockets for her cell phone. She didn't have it. Maybe she had lost it in the fire last night. She grabbed the hospital door and whipped it open, intending to go down to the nurse's station.

Wait! They are going to give you a hard time about being up. They are going to want to discharge you and that will take forever. Or worse they will want you to stay. Best if you do this subtly. Remember you came in on a helicopter last night after being unconscious for 10 minutes in the middle of a wildfire. Nobody is going to let you just walk out of here if they can help it.

Briefly her mind flashed to the man she had saved, wondering how he was. No time for that now.

She walked over to the phone by the bedside and dialed the number for the nurse's station. A cool female voice answered.

"Hi, it's Emma in 412. Did I get any visitors while I was sleeping?"

"No, Emma, none."

"Ok, thank you."

Emma broke the connection without replacing the handle and then dialed 9 for an outside line and Craig's number.

She sucked in her breath, counting the rings and silently praying he would pick up. After 7 rings his voicemail answered.

She slammed down the phone, biting her

tongue to keep from swearing or screaming, she wasn't sure which.

What now? Call dispatch and ask where he is.

It was a good idea, but she had to get out of the room before a nurse came in and saw her looking like she was just going to walk out of here, which was in fact what she was going to do.

She went to the door and opened it swiftly, walking towards the exit without hesitation. If anyone challenged her she would just keep walking. They weren't cops, just doctors and nurses.

She made it to the stairs without anyone even looking at her. Yanking the door open and swiftly stepping inside she sighed in relief. Once she was off this floor nobody would pay her any attention.

At the bottom floor she looked around for a pay phone. Why weren't there any around? Sometimes cellphone batteries die or are left in cars!

The emergency room had pay phones! She broke into a run, feeling like time was already running out for Craig. She had just gotten Craig back last night. She couldn't bear to think she had lost him again already.

She found a pay phone in the lobby and dug in her firefighter's uniform for a quarter. She called dispatch. Lindy answered.

"Lindy, it's Emma Hill. I need to know when the last time you heard from Firefighter 465 was."

"Hi Emma, how are you?"

The concern in Lindy's voice was obvious, but Emma didn't have time for it right now.

"I'm great Lindy, please look quickly, I'm really worried about him."

"Um well, he hasn't been heard from on the radio since his in service last night, but the scene commander already knows that."

Emma was confused.

"What do you mean he hasn't been heard from on the radio?"

Now Lindy sounded confused. "Emma, don't you know that there's a search on for him right now?"

Emma's heart sank. Her worst fears were confirmed.

"No Lindy, what is going on?"

"Well he disappeared last night on the line. One minute he was there and the next he wasn't. They've been searching for him since 5 this morning. The helicopters are up and everything. They just called and asked for police dogs, but those are going to take 6 hours to get here from Brickersville."

"Thanks Lindy," Emma said weakly. She replaced the handset, but held onto the phone still. She felt like she was going to fall to the ground in a heap if she let go. She couldn't get enough air.

Oh Craig, Craig, where are you? What happened?

Emma's vision went black around the edges. Her life spiraled out of her control in one sentence. She loved this man and he didn't even know it. Never would know it if he was ... she couldn't say it - couldn't even think it. He was fine, where ever he was - he just needed to be found.

She was going to help search. What else could she do? But how? She didn't have her car. How was she going to get up there?

As she thought, her eyes tracked movement in the E.R. doors. A worker bringing lab samples in. He had a car! And it was probably still running outside the doors - those guys were on a very tight schedule.

Emma Hill, are you considering stealing a car?

Emma thought about it hard. Was she really considering it? Well, yeah, anything else would take too long. Every second she spent here was a second Craig could be dy- *Don't say it! He's fine!*

Emma could actually feel her brain starting to crack under the strain. The need to be on the move right now felt so great she was surprised she was still standing stock still thinking and not running around in circles or pulling out her hair in a cartoonish display of angst.

There was no one here at the hospital that she could think of who would lend her a car without a lot of explanation. What about the courtesy cars in the garage? She knew where the keys were kept - in the volunteer's office near medical records. She'd once helped a volunteer walk an elderly person out to one of the cars and had thought how cool it was that the hospital had them.

So how to get the keys? She knew a few of the volunteers from coming in and out of the hospital so often but she didn't know any of them well. She was in uniform, so that gave her a certain air of authority - maybe she could just bluff her way in and act like she had been ordered to take a car.

She mulled this over as she walked towards the volunteer's office. When she got there, the desk in front was empty and the door behind was open. Yes! This would make things so much easier!

She slipped behind the desk and walked in the office, turning to the peg board on the left behind the door. 2 sets of keys stood there. She grabbed the one with the stall 3b marked on it. As her hand touched the cool metal her heart skipped a beat in her chest. She'd never stolen anything in her life. *Borrowed, I am just borrowing.* She slipped out of the office, face red and eyes darting over the lobby. She walked quickly towards the parking garage, thinking *I swear I will return these as soon as I can, please don't let anyone need it or notice it missing.*

She found the stall in the parking garage and slipped into the small white hatchback, cranking the ignition as soon as she got inside. Quickly, she pulled out of the stall and headed to the exit, strapping on her seatbelt as she drove.

A short line of cars formed in front of her. Damn! What was the exit security guard going to do? Was she caught already? She was no good at this clandestine stuff. A sheen of sweat covered her forehead and back. She felt nausea spike her empty stomach. Her mind played a silent film reel for her of the security guard dropping the gate down in front of her, looking suspiciously at her, then picking up the phone and making a call. In her mind's eye she pressed her lips together and lowered her head, gunning the engine. She saw herself ramming the gate and breaking it like in the movies. Her mind showed her fleeing up Crystal Mountain Road with police officers on her tail, shooting at her tires.

Emma grabbed the wheel tight enough to snap it off and forced herself to take a deep, steadying breath. She tried to push the images away. They wouldn't go. She brought in a new image. Craig. Craig's dimpled smile. Craig kissing her outside his truck on their first date. Craig rushing to pick her up at the Coronado after the fiasco with that asshole doctor.

She pulled up to the guardhouse and tried to smile at the guard. He smiled at her and raised the gate, giving her a small salute.

Emma let out a shaky breath and waved two fingers at him. She pressed the accelerator a little too hard making the car jerk forward. *Oh man, better get out of here quick.*

She forced herself to take a few more deep breaths and headed left in front of the hospital. She could be to the fire scene in 40 minutes if she hurried. Time to see what this little car could do.

Chapter 2

Once out of the city limits Emma pushed the little car to its limits, no longer concerned about police. As she drove she started wondering about Norman. Had he done something to Craig? And then he came in to gloat about it to her? But that didn't make sense. Wouldn't that be stupid of him? Because if Craig had been assaulted or something, now Emma would know who did it? Maybe he just had heard that Craig was missing and that's what he was gloating about. That things always seemed to fall apart for her and the men she tried to date, whether he had any part in it or not.

Emma tried to push the thoughts of Norman out of her head. Even after Norman had hit her, she still hadn't hated him. Hate was not one of those emotions she liked to nurture. She thought hate was too dangerous. Even after Norman had chased off all the men she'd tried to date she still never thought of him hatefully. She just kind of gave up, went numb, stopped trying.

But now, now she was starting to feel hate for Norman. And she didn't like the feeling. It was like acid in her body, burning her from the inside.

She tried to think of a strategy instead. Craig had come up to fight the wildfire last night just like she had yesterday. She was certain he would have been assigned a partner, and then sent out with a shovel to put out spot fires and maybe do some back burning. This is much trickier at night, but it had to be done still with a wildfire that was threatening homes.

They were probably doing a police call kind of search, where everyone walked in a line a few feet apart and looked straight at the ground. They probably expected that he had been overcome by smoke or maybe had tripped and hit his head (like she had the night before, with help from that big, falling tree) and so be passed out on the ground somewhere.

She heard the whoop whoop of a helicopter and leaned over the steering wheel, searching for it. There - she saw it circling in the distance, past the green, intact forest she currently saw on her left, over the blackened, charred hillside. He should be fairly easy to spot from the air in his orange fire suit, unless he was in the trees somewhere. The Crystal Creek Wildfire seemed to be out, at least in this location. She saw only the faintest wisps of smoke here and there.

She passed her first empty, parked fire vehicle pulled to the side on the two-land blacktop so she started watching for the scene commander. The commander today would probably be Captain Lane. Emma really liked Captain Lane, but she was also worried. Captain Lane was tough and Emma didn't know if the captain would give her a hard time about being there or not.

There - she saw her. Captain Lane was not your typical fire captain. She was a woman, for one, and she looked like she belonged on a movie set, not a fire scene. She stood 5 feet, 11 inches and had an hourglass figure even bulky turnout gear couldn't hide. Her flaming red hair sometimes made her seem made for the job though. She was standing with her foot on the back of a tanker, wearing a dingy gray t-shirt, firefighter turnout pants and boots, and a wildfire helmet on her head with all of her hair tucked inside, although a few long strands had escaped and made her easy to spot. She had a clipboard in one hand and was barking orders into the radio in her other hand.

Emma parked the hatchback and got out, running over to the captain. She had no idea what she was going to say; she was just glad to be here finally.

She waited until the captain was done speaking and then said "Captain, put me to work, I want to help find Masterson."

Captain Lane's eyes narrowed. "Hill, aren't you supposed to be in the hospital?"

"I was released this morning. I got a clean bill of health and plenty of sleep so I'm back to work."

Captain Lane eyed her clipboard. "Nobody told me you were coming."

"Well I was scheduled to work today before my, uh, my accident."

"Yeah, you were, but you were also yanked from the roster once you got med-evaced out of here last night in a helicopter," the Captain said tersely. Then she warmed up a little, "Good work by the way, I heard how you saved that hunter."

"Thanks Captain, but I'm here and I'm fine and I want to go to work." Emma tried not to shout, but her low-level anxiety was ratcheting back up to high level anxiety. She tried a different tactic. "Where are we searching for him?"

Captain Lane appraised her intently, seeming to peer inside Emma's eyes. *She's probably checking my color*, Emma thought.

The Captain turned to the south side of the road and waved off to the right. "We have 6 bodies and a heli searching this hillside right here. If they don't find him we head into the forest. If they still don't find him we have dogs on their way."

"When did he go missing? And how?"

"Shortly after 5 a.m. Tanner, his partner, noticed he just disappeared. He sounded the alarm and we did a spiral from their area. Nothing. Since then we've searched every sector on the south side of the road except the far forest. We haven't found anything."

"Why aren't there more bodies up here searching? And another helicopter? We could cover twice as much ground." Emma tried not to sound accusing, but it had been 6 hours already. 6 bodies and one helicopter was ridiculous!

"I asked for more bodies and got denied. I asked for another helicopter and got denied there too," the captain spit out.

Emma chose her words carefully. "Maybe we should go to the chief."

Captain Lane moved in close to Emma. "Don't you think I tried that! Those denials came straight from the Chief's mouth. He said he checked the manpower himself and there was no one to spare."

Emma's eyes widened. It was daytime, there were probably 20 firefighters working on this fire in other areas. All of them could come over here. No houses were currently being threatened. What in the world?

"What about the volunteers?"

Captain Lane sighed. "Look Emma, if this gets out, it's going to get me fired, but I've already made my bed so I'll tell you. I asked the chief for volunteers and he said the last thing he needed was 5 volunteers going missing because one paid firefighter couldn't tell his ass from a hole in the ground. He denied that request too. I didn't like his answer so I put the word out an hour ago that if some volunteers happened to show up to the fire there might be some jobs for them. I expect them to start showing up any minute now, and when they do I'll put them to work. And if any of them get lost or hurt I will certainly be fired. But that's better than just standing around."

Emma couldn't believe the chief wouldn't pull manpower from anywhere else and he wouldn't send up the volunteers. It was almost like he didn't care if Craig was found or not.

Emma thought hard. "What if there was foul play? Like what if someone hit him over the head or something? Shouldn't the woods be the first place you looked?"

Captain Lane eyed her carefully again. "Why would you think there was foul play?"

Emma didn't know whether to spill her guts or not. Accusing a Vice Captain in the police department of making someone go missing was serious business. And she didn't have anything to go on, just a mockingly-said sentence and a gut feeling. So she made something up.

"Craig told me last week that he had gotten a threatening letter and didn't know who it was from, so maybe someone took advantage of the fire to get some sort of revenge," she said, haltingly. She was a horrible liar and she knew it.

Captain Lane looked out over the barren hillside, and then over to the forest, which was over a mile away from where the current search was on.

"But Craig is a big guy. How would someone get him over to the forest from where he was working last night?" she asked, almost to herself.

"I don't know. But I want to go search the forest," Emma replied.

"Ok. When the first volunteer gets here you go with him."

"No, I don't want to wait. I'll go in now. Just give me a radio and a flare gun."

Captain Lane looked at her reproachfully. "You know better than that Emma, no one goes in without a partner."

Damn. Now she had to wait? The thought made her bounce up and down on her heels, impatiently. "Pull someone from the current search and send them in with me."

Captain Lane stood still, considering. "I should go with you myself, but if I did there would be no one here to tell the volunteers what to do when they start showing up. Ok - I'll give you Tanner. He won't go home anyway."

Emma sighed with relief. Her heart was still hammering and she didn't feel any better about anything - wouldn't feel better until Craig was found - but at least she would be moving again.

Captain Lane yelled into her radio. Emma started searching vehicles for spare aid bags, wildfire kits, water bottles, radios, and flare guns. When she found what she needed she strapped it all to her back and started towards the woods, looking for Tanner. She saw him cutting across the charred hillside and waved a big wave, then kept moving. As she passed the Captain she said, "Tell Tanner to switch to channel 18."

She jogged the 3/4s of a mile to the start of the forest. She was sure Tanner was exhausted but she didn't need him to keep up with her. Her nervous energy would do the work of two of them anyway. She tied off a length of orange tape on a tree where she entered and plunged ahead. She'd always had a pretty good intuition when it came to this kind of work. When she got in the zone she just 'knew' where she should be going and what she should be doing and most times exactly what was wrong with her patient even if it wasn't obvious. She shut down her thinking mind and started to feel around for her sixth sense, hoping desperately it wouldn't fail her today when she needed it the most.

Her radio crackled. "Emma where are

you?"

"Follow the orange tape Tan, I'm already looking."

She placed another orange strip quickly and kept moving.

The forest was dark and cool and eerily still. There were no squirrels or birds or chipmunks to be seen or heard. They had all fled the night before when the fire threatened so close, she was sure.

A picture formed in her mind. A hunting shack. The shack from last night where she had found the hunter? Or another? She cast her eyes around the forest looking for any sort of a building. "Craig!" she called suddenly, startling herself. No answer.

She kept walking, feeling a kind of deja vu from the night before, except this time the forest wasn't on fire.

The forest opened up into an unnatural clearing. She saw a deer blind up in a tree, camouflaged well. She placed another piece of tape, then picked up her pace, thinking there would be some more hunting buildings around this area. The smell of old smoke mingled with fresh pine trees, creating an inviting aroma that didn't mesh well with her situation. Every step felt surreal. The unnatural quiet allowed her to hear every footfall she made and the sound of her own swishing heartbeat in her ears. She didn't like it. She wished something, anything would make a noise. Weren't there even any bugs left here?

The forest got too thick ahead of her to

continue that way so she placed some tape and veered to the left. She walked for at least a half-mile. Soon she would come to the far end of what was left of the non-burnt forest. And then what? Would she circle around and find another place of entry and just walk like she had here?

She came upon another unnatural clearing. All the trees had been cut down, but there was a charred pile of wood on the far side of it. Had that been a hunters shack? She ran up to it. The big planks of wood were ashy and sooty, some of them burned more than halfway through. Her heart pounded harder. Someone had set this wood on fire, certainly - had it once been a building? Was she going to find a dead body in the middle of it? "Please no please no please no" she started chanting under her breath without even realizing it.

She tested the first board. It was cool to the touch. She pulled it off the pile and threw it off to the side. Frantically now, she dug at the boards, heaving them as fast and as far as she could. The wood at the bottom started to change. It wasn't quite as burnt. Some of the pieces didn't look burnt at all.

There! A flash of orange! Emma whimpered and made a low keening sound, like an animal. He was dead. She knew it. Someone had put him in this little shack and set it on fire. "Craig!" she screamed, whipping into a frenzy. She heaved the planks off him with all her might, uncovering his boots, and then his hips, and then his chest. He wasn't moving. She kept digging and when the final pieces were flung away she took in the sight of him.

He was lying, face down, helmet still on, in a pool of his own congealed blood. His turnout gear was charred on the back in places, but not burnt through anywhere. The fire hadn't gotten him when the building collapsed in on him. He must not have died immediately because she saw he had dug a little hole in the dirt by his mouth with his fingers. A sob escaped her. She dropped to her knees next to him, eyes filled with tears. He had saved her. She could not save him.

Her fingers, strictly by habit, snuck to his neck. She felt for his pulse without realizing she was doing it. A light flutter played over her fingertips.

"Oh my God Craig, you're alive, Craig, hang in there my sweet. I am going to get you out of here."

She stood up. "Tanner!" She screamed, shredding her vocal cords. A moment later, he burst into the clearing, a look of terror on his face.

"Emma, what!? What is it?!"

"Tanner, I found him. Oh God he's alive. Get the helicopter over here."

He grabbed for his radio. Emma turned back to Craig, praying he would live long enough to get med-evaced out in the helicopter.

Chapter 3

Norman packed up his binoculars and headed for the exit. He was satisfied the Sea Cafe was not being watched so his weekly pre-meeting sweep was over. He walked down the stairs of the insurance building, out the exit and across the street to the restaurant.

"Table for one, Sir?" the host asked.

Norman pulled out his badge. "I'll seat myself," he said in his gruff, ask-no-questions-and-I-won't-hurt-you voice and kept on walking, ignoring the host's confused look.

He stood in the archway and eyed the room. People looked his way immediately. He always cut an imposing figure - standing 6 foot 2 inches tall, but he was unlikely to be recognized in this get up. He wore something different every time they had one of these meetings. It was becoming more like a game to him every time he went out and bought a new outfit. This one was one of his favorites. A dark blue suit with a bolero tie, complete with cowboy hat low over his eyes and cowboy boots on his feet. He felt like Clint Eastwood.

He saw the Senator seated in the back, near the wall. Good, there was an empty table close by. He walked to it and sat down, opening the menu.

The waiter came by. Before he could say a word Norman held up his menu and growled,

"Snapper and salsa. Your finest craft beer. Don't come back till it's all ready." The waiter swallowed, took the menu, and left quickly.

He sat back and relaxed, a satisfied smile on his face. It had been a good day. A very productive day. A fun day. He still had his old Navy Seal skills and they had bagged him one big fireman this morning. Norman laughed to himself. The Navy had given him a dishonorable discharge and a short jail term back in 2000, but they couldn't erase all the ways they had taught him to disable and kill a man. And thanks to a very good, very discreet hacker friend, all record of that jail term had been erased and the dishonorable discharge was turned into an honorable one. No one could prove it had ever even happened, especially since the judge who sentenced him plus the commanding officer who charged him were dead.

Now add one more to the body count. Norman often joked with himself that he was going to lose track of all the people he had killed someday. That fucking firefighter had been easy to kill. Muscles don't matter when you get shot 3 times. Firefighter. Ha, that was a good one. Norman knew he was FBI, investigating the death of Lucy Kinkaid. When the Senator started asking him to kill people, Norman did it, but he always investigated their back-trail, just so he never again got a nasty surprise like this one. Lucy's brother was FBI, and Lucy's fiance was FBI, which really pissed Norman off when he found out. What was the Senator playing at? Killing family members of the FBI. Not smart.

Honestly, though, the Senator probably didn't even know. He was stupid that way. He didn't weigh the pros and cons of his actions. He just eliminated anyone who was a threat in the quickest way possible. Norman often thought that if the Senator hadn't found him to do the dirty work he'd have been exposed already. Norman was smart and he knew how to cover his trail.

When he had first seen Craig *Masterson* (Craig MacDonnell actually) at Emma's house he knew he had seen that face before and it was important. His memory for detail had not failed him, and the next morning he woke up remembering where. He looked up the FBI academy picture to be sure, and then had his hacker friend figure out where he was assigned. The friend could find nothing - only that he was undercover. *Undercover here in Westwood Harbor.* It was actually good luck that the bastard had been interested in Emma, otherwise he might never have been tipped off. Then all he had to do was decide what to do with him. This wildfire had been a blessing. He'd had a reliable tail on Masterson for days and when he'd heard he was going to be at the wildfire at night he decided to take advantage. A gun in the back had convinced Craig to move, and then a few bullets had convinced him to lie down. Norman had set the building on fire and watched for a few trees to go up too, and then got out of there fast. By now, the whole area should be nothing but ash. Who knew if they would even find the body? And since the whole area was on fire anyway, it wouldn't even look suspicious.

Norman's thoughts were interrupted by movement at the Senator's table. Senator Oberlin got up and walked past him on the way to the bathroom, dropping a small piece of dark paper on his table as he passed. Norman palmed it immediately. He watched the Senator walk to the bathroom. Expensive 3 piece suit, balding on top, still trim and strong. He had to be what, pushing 70 years old? Norman hoped he took care of himself. The Senator had promised him Chief within 10 years for doing all the dirty work that couldn't be trusted to ordinary criminals. The Senator never wanted to hear details, just that the job was done. Norman thought he liked to pretend his hands were cleaner that way.

Norman's food came, and he ate it quickly, mopping up his sauce with his bread and drinking the beer in one swallow. He threw 2 bills on the table and left without a word to anyone.

Once in his car he unfolded the Senator's note.

C.N. needs another lesson. Your choice. H-job. See details you know where. Maricio's.

So Chuck Nance was going to have another 'accident' befall him. OK. He'd have to think of something a little more creative than blowing up his factory, setting fire to his house, and loosening the lug nuts on his wife's car. Either that man had the stubbornness of a mule, or the brains of one. Norman didn't know what Senator Oberlin wanted from Nance, but he didn't much care either. He just wanted that

Chief's position. And he didn't mind fucking with people's lives in the slightest.

And H-job. Apparently there was another hacker job the Senator needed done, modifying records or something. That was fine, as long as there was cold hard cash sitting alongside those details. His friend didn't work cheap.

And Maricio's. Next week's meeting would be at the same time on the same day, just a different restaurant. Norman thought maybe he'd go in biker gear next time. Maybe a black doo-rag over his head and a leather jacket and chaps. Too bad he didn't have time to grow a beard. Maybe he could even commandeer a Harley to ride in on.

Norman started to get excited thinking about it. Maybe he'd visit Nance in character in the middle of the night and slice off a finger or something. He shifted in his seat. Damn, his excitement was showing behind his zipper. Hmmm, maybe it was time to visit Lydia or Chloe.

He quickly committed all the details to memory and tore up the piece of paper in little pieces and dumped half of them out his window and put the other half in his ashtray, then started the car and pulled out into traffic.

Senator Oberlin wanted him to eat the pieces of paper and Norman said he did, just to appease him. But damned if he was going to actually do it. That was stupid. If he hadn't already had enough dirt on the good Senator to bury him 5 times over he would have saved every single paper, but as it was he didn't have to.

Like the Senator's first and possibly worst job ever (that Norman knew about). First screwing and then killing a 15 year old girl because she got pregnant with his babies. Norman knew about that one because it was the first hack job Senator Oberlin had ever given him. To erase all medical and autopsy records pertaining to the death of a Christie Callahan on September 13th, 1983. Norman had found the records: 15 year old girl brought to the hospital by a man who found her crawling, in labor, on the side of the road. She didn't say a word, just screamed. Blood was gushing out of her the whole time. The babies were delivered and were fine, but they were never able to stop the girl's bleeding. She died a Jane Doe, never even able to give her name.

At first, Norman hadn't found any records on a Christie Callahan dying that day. He checked the day before and the day after. Still finding nothing he looked up Christie herself. She had been reported a runaway in May of 1983. Case never closed. Norman found her mom and, pretending to still be looking into the case, he asked her some questions. It turned out that her mom suspected Christie had run off with an older man - one who looked almost 40. Christie's mom didn't remember much about what he looked like, but she shared what she did remember. She had seen them together once and confronted Christie about it but Christie wouldn't tell her anything. The day before she ran away, her mom had accused her of being pregnant. Her shape was changing and her breasts were growing. Christie had left the house crying, come back that night, and left the next day for school but just never returned. Christie's mom told all the details mechanically. Norman could tell she thought her girl was dead and had for a long time. Norman didn't tell her she was right.

Norman went back to his hacker friend and had him check records on any Jane Does that had died that day. There it was. 15 year old Christie had died from bleeding out during delivery, and the doctor had not noted anything suspicious in the chart. An autopsy had never been done.

Norman reported back to the Senator the records were wiped. The senator searched his eyes for any accusation. Norman had none. What about the baby? the senator wanted to know. It died, Norman said, not sure why. I wiped that record too. Satisfied, the Senator had nodded, and given him another job.

Norman was interested in finding out what had happened to the babies. Adoption and foster system. Only one had stayed in Westwood Harbor. Norman followed the trail and found her. Named Emma Hill by the delivering nurse, and put into the foster system immediately, she was an exemplary Paramedic/Firefighter. Norman was curious, so he arranged a 'chance' meeting at work one day. She had inherited the Senator's light blue eyes, but not his dirty ways. She was a sweet, clean woman. The only woman he'd ever met who he couldn't see that dirty, waxy layer under her skin. He courted her, pulling out every charming trick he'd ever read in books and on websites. It worked. But he couldn't hold it together and they divorced soon after. Norman had his friend wipe that record of their marriage too. When Emma agreed to marry him again he wanted it to be like the first time. Like the only time.

On auto-pilot, Norman had made it all the way to his 'office-away-from-the-office'. His erection had made it too. He smiled. He was about to get out of the car when his cell phone rang. He listened, and his smile got wider. The tail on Emma had found a good reason to pull her over. "Perfect. Make sure she is fingerprinted." he said.

Then he got out of the car and walked inside, hoping both Lydia and Chloe would be there. He had a lot of celebrating to do.

Chapter 4

Emma didn't usually know how she felt about God. Her childhood had been just horrible enough for her to wonder if she had been abandoned by God, if indeed God existed. But that didn't matter right now. Sometimes she prayed under her breath, just a whispered "Please God" but today she said entire prayers, cobbled together from what she had seen on TV and heard from friends. She had a least 40 minutes till she made it to the hospital to see how Craig was, and that was a long time to sit and do nothing but drive.

She sped down the highway in her borrowed car and prayed to a God she desperately hoped was listening. She prayed for Craig and prayed for an answer to the questions that were plaguing her. She had told the helicopter to land right in the clearing they were in. It was too dangerous to try to move Craig far. He had lost a ton of blood by the look of the puddle he was laying in. While they were waiting for the helicopter she had turned him over and tried to asses his injuries. The hole in his turnout jacket suggested he was shot. But why would someone shoot Craig? Why would *Norman* shoot Craig? Would he really go to those lengths to keep her from dating?

She had opened up Craig's turnout gear and cut open his shirt to assess the damage. But there was none on the front. He was wearing a bulletproof vest. A much lighter and thinner bulletproof vest than the one she had always seen Norman put on. Emma's mind had swirled with questions. Why would Craig wear a bulletproof vest to a wildfire? Or ever?

But that meant the blood probably wasn't from a bullet wound in his chest? Her fingers had crept to his face, which was bathed in his blood. Underneath it, his skin felt smooth, but swollen. She'd felt around his ears and back to the back of his neck and head. His helmet was still on. She didn't dare take it off at this point. She hadn't noticed any holes in it from the back but she was starting to get scared it was keeping his skull together. In the back of his neck on the right side she'd found a large, bloody, scabbed over lump. Gingerly she'd probed its edges. Was this a bullet hole? Emma's paramedic brain had taken over, shoving the rest of her brain into a corner, where it cried like a small child.

As she had heard the chopper come close, and felt its buffeting winds, she felt Craig's pulse again at his neck. Fluttery, faint, but there. She'd cut his pants open up the right leg and checked the pulse near his groin. Nothing there. That was bad. That was very bad. That's when she had begun praying. When the chopper landed she gave the medic on board a report - what little she knew. She'd helped Tanner and the medic get Craig onto a board and as the two men carried him she had cut both of the sleeves to his jacket all the way to the collar so the medic could try to start an IV line in the air. She'd squeezed his hand and whispered in his ear "Please come back to me my love." And then he was gone.

She'd run all the way to her car and headed for the hospital.

Now, done reliving it again, she entered the city limits. A small voice told her to slow down, but she couldn't get her foot to let up on the pedal. She was desperate for news of Craig. Surely he was in surgery already. Westwood General had an amazing trauma center, and if anyone could save him, the doctors and nurses at Westwood General could.

She took the back way, hoping to run into less traffic. She pushed the small car to its limits on an open side street. She didn't look at the speedometer, but she heard the protesting whine of the engine and let up a little.

Behind her, a black and white fell into pace with her, flipping on its flashing lights. She didn't notice. A short whoop came from that direction, to get her attention. She paid it no mind and focused on the road ahead of her. Then she heard the full police siren turn on and wail. She glanced in her rear-view mirror and her heart wept. *Not now. I can't handle this now.*

Briefly, she considered just continuing to drive. But that would end with her being hauled off in handcuffs once she got to the hospital. Frustration made her eyes water, and she pulled over.

Stopped, she wiped her eyes and took some deep breaths. Should she claim official business? She was in her fire gear. No. That wouldn't work. No one was allowed to speed in a civilian car. She better just tell the truth. When the officer got to her window she rolled it down quickly and started telling her side.

"Officer, I'm sorry I was speeding, please, you have to let me go. My boyfr - my fiance is in the hospital. He was just taken to Westwood General in a helicopter. I'm afraid he's going to die." She felt close to tears again and decided to go with it. It could only help her, she thought.

The officer just looked at her. She checked his name tag - Officer Jeffries. She looked pleadingly into his eyes, her prayers now changing from prayers for Craig to prayers that he would understand and let her go. Fantasies of a lights and siren police escort flashed through her head.

"Don't move," he admonished, and disappeared.

Emma gawked backwards at him. He was going to just leave her here? Was he writing her a ticket? What was going on?

She watched him in her rear-view mirror. He was on his cell phone.

He looked up and caught her watching him. He hung up the phone and started for her car. "Step out of the car please," he said when he got to her window.

Fear shot through Emma's body. He wasn't even going to ask for her license and registration? Had someone reported this car stolen?

She weighed her options. She didn't have any. Desperately her mind wondered if Norman could help her. *Yeah right*, came the reply.

The officer took a step back and put his hand down near his belt. Emma's eyes followed the hand. It was on his taser. *Oh God, this is bad.*

"I said, step out of the car, right now."

Emma opened the door and got out quickly. She didn't want to be tased. Or arrested.

Officer Jeffries stepped back to allow her to get out. "Put your hands on your head and walk to the front of the car ma'am."

She did, fear beating at her breastbone.

He walked directly in front of her and said "Stand up straight and face me." He pulled a pen out of his breast pocket and told her to follow the pen's movements with her eyes, but not move her head.

She realized he was testing her for impaired driving. Thank God. She could pass this.

He ran her through the motions and she was certain she passed each test with flying colors. In between tests she chanted "hurry, hurry, hurry," inside her head. She felt frantic with desire to get to the hospital to see if Craig was alive.

"Turn around and put your hands on the hood of the car," he admonished her.

"What? Why? Are you going to arrest me? I passed your tests."

He smiled what seemed to Emma a rather slimy and sly smile. "Actually, you were a little shaky on the field sobriety test. I'll need to have you blow in the Breathalyzer, but mine isn't working so you have to come to the station."

Emma couldn't believe her ears. Had to go

to the station? Was she arrested?

"Am-am I under arrest?" she forced out.

Officer Jeffries dropped his right hand across his body to his taser again. His slimy grin got a little wider. "I said, turn around and put your hands on the hood of the car."

Emma's mouth went dry. Something told her this man wanted to taze her. He was hoping she would give him a hard time. Thoughts of fear for Craig fled to the back of her brain and thoughts of fear for her own safety took over. She turned around and put her hands on the hood like instructed, her eyes searching the surrounding area for anyone who could help her, or at least be a witness to her "arrest".

They were just barely inside the city limits. The street was two lane in both directions and traffic was light. There were a few buildings on both sides of the road, but no foot traffic. Emma felt very vulnerable.

Officer Jeffries stuck his boot in between Emma's feet and kicked them 2 feet apart, hard. He put one foot behind her right leg and bent over, putting his hands around her right ankle, feeling her leg all the way from her ankle up to her thigh. She was being patted down for weapons. Emma felt sick. She'd seen officers do this many times, but never to her.

His hands were very aggressive. When he got to her groin he squeezed and rubbed her most intimate parts before heading back down the other leg. She jumped and gasped a little. Now she felt violated too. Emma's swirling thoughts began to jangle sharply together, paralyzing her. This was wrong. This was all wrong. But what could she do? If she ran he'd catch her and taze her and arrest her for sure. And he'd actually have something to arrest her for. Oh a dirty cop was the worst kind of criminal in the world, because they had so much authority. If this cop was a dirty cop, or one of Norman's friends, she could be in deep trouble.

Officer Jeffries stood up and started at her waist, patting up her sides. He put his hand on her breast and she couldn't help herself any longer. She grabbed his hand and screamed "Don't touch me!"

Jeffries chuckled behind her and said, "Wrong move sweetheart." He wrenched both her arms behind her back, handcuffing them in one swift move. Then he slammed her head down on the hood of the car. "You have the right to remain silent ..."

Emma squeezed her eyes shut. She couldn't believe what was going. She didn't hear her rights. She could only hear the blood pounding in her ears and her own voice chanting *why, why, why?* inside her mind.

***

Jeffries didn't say a word on the way to the station. Emma was half afraid he was going to drive her back out of the city limits and shoot her or something, but when she saw them draw close to the station she breathed a sigh of relief.

He hauled her roughly out of the car and steered her into the cell block area. Her mind raced frantically. She didn't even know what she was arrested for, but she didn't think asking Jeffries was going to get her anywhere.

He took her to a small room and took her fingerprints and her picture, all without a word except, "turn to your left, turn to your right." He seemed to delight in shoving her around. After processing he took her straight to the cell block and shoved her in the small door.

"Wait! What about my phone call!" she yelled, turning around and grabbing the bars. He grinned at her and walked out of the room.

She looked around hesitantly. The cell block was just a large, open cage inside a large, open room. There were at least 10 other women in with her, most sitting on the benches pushed towards the walls of the cage. All of them looking her up and down, many with judgmental or angry sneers on their faces - she couldn't tell which. On the other side of the room was a desk with an officer sitting at it doing paperwork. He didn't look up.

Emma looked desperately about for a phone. There were no phones in the room or the cage.

"Uh, anyone have a phone I could borrow?" she asked quietly.

A slim black woman wearing a pink boa and a purple body suit told her, "Nah sister, they don't let us have phones in here."

Emma backed against the bars, and slid to the ground, dropping her head in her hands. This couldn't possibly get any worse.

She looked back up at the woman and

almost whispered, "But they have to let me make a phone call right?"

The woman laughed, a short barking laugh. "You never been arrested before?"

Emma shook her head no.

"Course not. You firewomen don't get arrested much, or did you steal that suit?"

"It's mine."

The woman laughed again. "They don't have to give you a phone call 'less they charge you with something. If you just arrested, there ain't nobody you can call that can do nothin for you anyway."

"I don't think I'm charged with anything. How long until they charge me?"

"They can keep you here for 2 days before they have to let you go or charge you with somethin."

Emma dropped her head into her hands again. She couldn't believe this. She had no idea if Craig was dead or alive, and the police could keep here for 2 days? And then just let her go like nothing ever happened if they wanted to? *Think Emma, think!* Maybe she could ask to talk to one of the cops she knew from paramedic work. Maybe somebody would be willing to help her or make some calls for her.

Emma looked down the room at the officer at the desk. She didn't think she knew him. She was trying to think of the highest ranking officer she knew when a door opened in the room. Officer Jeffries came back in, holding the elbow of another woman. She had messy, long brown hair and a pretty face with a lot of makeup. She was wearing a tight black miniskirt and a tight pink halter top. Emma thought she recognized the woman from somewhere, but couldn't place her.

Jeffries opened the door and motioned the woman into the cell. She looked at him and nodded and walked in a few steps, then turned around and watched the officer. He walked to the man at the desk and said, "Hey Curt, I need your help with something."

"What?" Curt answered.

"I need your help with some records in the records room."

"Ok, get someone to watch the cell and I'll be right there."

"I've got the guard watching on the cameras already."

Curt grunted and got up and followed Jeffries out of the room. The new woman watched them go.

As soon as they were gone she prodded Emma with her foot. "Hey you bitch, get up, that's my seat."

Emma looked up at her incredulously. "What? This is the floor."

"Yeah, that's my spot on the floor. Move your ass somewhere else."

Emma didn't want to get into any fights. She got to her feet and tried to edge around the woman. The woman watched her and then put her hand into her bra, pulling out a small, pink boxcutter. The blade glinted wickedly.

Emma's eyes widened and her heart felt like it was going to pound straight out of her chest. She put her hands out in front of her. She'd picked up people in the ambulance before who had been sliced with boxcutters. They were a gang weapon mostly.

"Look, I don't want any trouble," she said, taking a step back.

She must have backed right into someone because she felt hands shoving her back forwards. Her eyes flicked to the woman who she had spoken with earlier for help. No help there - she had backed up to the far corner of the cellblock, her eyes wide and focused on the boxcutter too.

The new woman held the boxcutter in her right hand and held her left hand up too, and she bent over a bit, looking like she was about to pounce on Emma.

"Well then if you don't want any trouble, maybe you shouldn't start no trouble," the woman said, stepping closer to Emma. Emma couldn't go backwards, so she went sideways one step.

"Ok, Ok, I won't start no trouble," she said.

The woman took one more step forward. "Seems you already did or you wouldn't be gettin this lesson, now would you. Your lesson is to keep your mouth shut and do what you are told."

Emma tried to follow the conversation. Keep her mouth shut? Do what she was told? Did someone send this crazy woman in here to tell her that?

The woman lunged forward, the box cutter slicing through the air towards Emma's face. Emma leaned backwards out of the way quickly.

The woman rushed her, silently. Emma wasn't expecting it and down they went. Emma didn't feel cut. Her eyes desperately searched out the boxcutter. It was buried in her thick turnout jacket sleeve. Thank God she still had it on.

The woman straddled her and sliced again, aiming for Emma's chest. Emma grabbed both her hands and twisted as hard as she could. Dimly, she was aware of screaming in the room.

The woman didn't let go, but clawed at Emma's hands with her other hand and twisted the box cutter, slicing into the back of Emma's left hand and down her wrist.

Hot fire burned across her skin. The pain was bad, but Emma barely noticed it. She twisted as hard as she could, trying to get the other woman to let go of the weapon.

Emma heard a loud pop sound and the woman suddenly pitched forward towards her, her hand going limp. Emma wrenched the boxcutter out of her hand and slid it across the floor quickly. Only then did she realize the room was silent and her attacker was motionless on the ground. She looked up. Two cops were standing at the entrance to the cellblock, one of them holding a shotgun. Neither of them was Jeffries.

Emma's heart was pounding with exertion and fear and her breaths were tearing in and out of her throat. Had they shot that woman? Emma didn't see any blood on her. Then she saw what she thought was a beanbag. Oh, they had shot her with a beanbag gun.

The cop with the shotgun pointed at her. "You, come here."

She got shakily to her feet and walked to him. Adrenaline made her feel light headed.

He took her by the elbow and walked her out of the cellblock and out of the room to another small room just outside the door. Blood dripped from her wrist and left a grisly trail from the cellblock into the small room. The officer gave her some tissues from the desk and told her to sit down.

"I'm going to call the medics to come treat you. When I come back you can tell me what happened."

Emma nodded and sat down, holding compression on the slice on her hand and wrist. A subtle click told her she was locked in.

A phone! The desk had a phone on it. Emma grabbed the receiver and punched in Jerry's cell number quickly, ignoring the pain in her arm.

He answered. "Jerry, I'm at the police station. I got arrested. Somebody cut me. Craig is at the hospital. Jerry you gotta come get me!"

Emma collapsed into tears for the hundredth time that day.

Chapter 5

"Jerry , I can't believe you did that! You could lose your job!" Emma whispered urgently as soon as the rear ambulance doors shut, cutting their low voices off from any police officers in the parking lot.

"Some things are more important than my job Em, like what's right, and good friends. Besides, I'm not going to lose my job. That is a pretty nasty cut, even if it didn't graze any arteries."

Jerry had jumped the ambulance call to the cellblock for Emma, telling central dispatch he was right around the corner. He was working with Beth this time since Emma had taken wildfire duty. Jerry and Emma both liked and trusted Beth, one of the oldest and spiciest Paramedics in the department at 59. Beth could have had the supervisor position or even a Lieutenant's or Captain's position at any time, but she stayed in the trenches where she liked it best. She even preferred to float instead of work with a regular partner. She loved people, and she was a pure adrenaline junkie.

When Beth and Jerry got to the police station, Emma was telling Officer Cade what had happened. Officer Cade was calm and sympathetic, writing everything she said down into his little notebook. His manner and his kind brown eyes had relaxed Emma. Why couldn't all cops be like this?

Jerry didn't act like he knew Emma when he came in, he just got down to business. He had looked at her hand and immediately wrapped it up tight. He had turned to Officer Cade and said, "She needs to be transported quickly. That cut nicked an artery. Is she released or are you coming with us?"

Cade had looked flustered. "She's not my prisoner. Can you wait 2 minutes?"

"If it's any more than 2 minutes we're just going to take her."

Cade had rushed out of the room.

Emma and Jerry had had a quick, whispered conversation in which she learned Craig had been in surgery an hour before but the hospital wouldn't say anything else. She gave Jerry the short version of how she had ended up in the cellblock. Jerry was livid for her. Beth didn't say anything, but her face gave away her anger at what seemed to be Emma's wrongful arrest.

Officer Jeffries had then entered the room, causing Emma to shrink back on herself. She didn't want to be scared of him but she was.

He had made it pretty clear he didn't believe that Emma was badly hurt but his Sergeant had made him release her pending investigation. He had made her sign a form and given her a large manila envelope and left the room.

Emma, Jerry, and Beth had practically run out of there.

***

When they got to Westwood General Emma barreled out of the ambulance, wanting to run straight up to the surgical center or the ICU and start looking for Craig.

"Wait, Emma, wait. If we don't get that hand cleaned up you are going to get a nasty infection or worse. Look, it will only take 5 minutes."

"No Jerry, I'll do it later, I gotta find Craig."

Jerry looked to Beth for help.

"Emma," Beth said. "Let Jerry clean you up. I'll start calling around and figure out where he is and what's going on. It will be faster than you just running around with no idea where to go."

Emma knew they were right. They ducked into a trauma room and Jerry spent a few minutes cleaning the cut out well and then gluing it shut with skin glue. He bandaged it up tight and admonished her to keep a close eye on it for infection.

Emma watched the door the whole time for Beth's return. True to her word, she was back in 4 minutes.

"He's in the ICU, room 1214 but no visitors allowed, and no word on how he is."

"Perfect, thanks Beth, they'll let me in," Emma said, sighing her relief. He had made it through surgery.

As Jerry was cleaning up the mess they

had made, his radio crackled. Dispatch was swamped with calls and not enough available paramedics.

"Looks like we are out of here Em, good luck." Jerry kissed her on the cheek. Beth gave a wave and a smile and they were out the door.

"Thanks guys!" Emma yelled after them. She took off at a jog to the elevator.

In the ICU, she rounded the corner towards room 1214 and saw two beefy looking men with short hair, wearing dark sports coats and dark pants sitting in uncomfortable-looking metal chairs in front of one of the doors. Emma immediately got an FBI vibe from them. Not that she knew a lot of FBI officers, but she watched TV. *How strange*, Emma thought. *Is that room 1214?*

As she got closer she could tell it was. She had planned on just walking in the room like she belonged, not stopping at the nurse's station for permission. Well, maybe that would still work.

She walked up to the men and said "Excuse me, I need to get inside."

The men looked at her. "No one gets inside but the doctor and the nurse," the man on the left said.

Crap! What now? She was getting inside that room, she didn't care what it took.

"Look, I'm his fiance, I need to get in the room and just check on him."

The men exchanged glances. The one on the right smiled a little and crossed his arms. The one on the left was the spokesman apparently. He said, "Our orders are no one gets inside but the doctor and the nurse. Not even fiances."

"Well who are you? Orders from who? What gives you that right?" Emma demanded, feeling very put out at this information.

The man on the left sighed and stood up. He was only a bit taller than Emma, but very wide through the chest, with thick, jet-black hair and a 5 o'clock shadow. He put his hand in his coat and pulled out a badge.

"We are FBI agents investigating the attempted murder of Craig Masterson. No one goes in but the doctor and the nurse. Period." He spoke the period with finality and leaned forward getting in her face a little.

Emma hated confrontation, but when she got upset she could go toe to toe with anyone. And she was getting very upset. This *agent* didn't have a clue what she had been through to get here.

"Look, I want to see my fiance. Just for a second. I won't hurt him, and I won't try to kill him. You can come in with me. Just let me in!" She kept her voice low so it didn't carry to the nurses station, but mustered every bit of authority she had.

"No."

Emma thought for a second. She didn't have the energy to flirt, and that wouldn't work anyway. She could go away and steal a nurses uniform, but they'd already studied her face.

"I want to talk to your boss," she finally said.

"No."

"What do you mean no? You have to tell

me who your boss is. You are a public employee!"

The big man shrugged and sat down again.

Emma paced for a second. Then she came back to him, hands crossed over her chest to keep them from shaking. "Look. I saved him OK? He'd be dead if it weren't for me. There was nobody guarding him up at the wildfire. No one could even *find* him until I looked in the woods and found him. If it weren't for me he'd still be lying on the ground, covered with burnt wood, probably completely bled out!" Her whole body started to shake with the last few words. She didn't want to have to admit this to herself, much less say it to a complete stranger.

The two men exchanged a glance again, this one much more urgent than the first. The agent who hadn't spoken whipped a phone out of his breast pocket and made a phone call.

"We need you here," he said and hung up.

Emma looked from one face to the other. "Well?" she demanded.

"Just sit tight," the man with the phone said. "You'll get to meet our boss in a second."

The door at the end of the hall opened. They could all feel it and hear it but couldn't see anyone around the circular hallway yet. The two men sat up straight in their chairs. The one on the right stood up and crossed his arms over his chest. *Nervously?* Emma wondered.

Emma watched the hallway. Around the corner walked a wall of a man. He looked nothing like Craig, but reminded her of Craig anyway. Where Craig was fair this man was dark.

He was a bit over 6 feet tall, like Craig, and had a similar, muscular build. His jeans and form-fitting t-shirt were impeccably neat and crisp. He wore heavy workboots, but glided over the ground without making a sound.

The second agent walked over to him and said a few things in his ear, gesturing once to Emma. This new agent's eyes never left Emma's. She could feel them searching her very soul, demanding answers of who she really was. She squirmed a little, not liking the feeling. Most people took her at face value. She was cute, she was smart, and she was good. This man seemed to already think she was none of those things.

He walked over. "Miss Hill, my name is Agent Kinkaid. Would you come with me please?"

"To where? Why?" she retorted, not wanting to leave without at least getting a peek at Craig.

"To my office, so I can interview you regarding how you found Craig Masterson."

"I want to see him first." She mentally dug in her heels, preparing to insist.

He nodded his head slightly to the agent left in front of the door. The agent stood up and cleared a path. Emma couldn't believe it. She ran to the door and pushed it open.

The room smelled of antiseptic. It was small, only big enough for one bed, a chair, and a dizzying array of medical equipment. The beep beep beep of his heart monitor greeted her. *Regular*, her paramedic brain thought. She walked slowly over to the bed. He was covered with blankets and she couldn't see his face but she could tell already he had a breathing tube down his throat, taped to his face. Tears formed in her eyes.

She walked up to him and put her hand gently in his hair. His eyes were taped shut. The right side of his face was swollen and bandaged. The right side of his head was shaved and she saw another bandage near the back of his head where she'd felt the lump.

Her hands snuck down to his arm. His brachial pulse was strong. Good. She looked back at the door. Agent Kinkaid had followed her to the foot of the bed and was watching her intently, a strange, sad look on his face.

She checked the monitor for his heart rate, blood pressure, and oxygen saturation. They all looked good. She really wished she could get a look at his chart. She leaned over and whispered in his ear, "Craig, come back to me please." She stayed bent over for a moment, smelling his scent and willing him to stir.

Nothing.

She straightened. "I am ready," she said to Agent Kinkaid. "Thank you," she added as an afterthought.

He nodded and motioned her towards the door.

***

Emma followed Agent Kinkaid into a small, windowless room in the basement of the hospital. She sat down in the metal chair opposite a tiny desk with only a phone and some paper on it. "The hospital lent me this office to set up operations while we investigate this crime and protect Firefighter Masterson," he said, noticing Emma looking around in confusion.

Emma opened her mouth to ask why the FBI was involved but the Agent spoke again, quickly. "Tell me exactly how you found him. Don't leave anything out. Even the smallest detail could be important." He grabbed a pen and hovered his hand over a pad of paper on the table.

Emma thought back to this morning at 10 o'clock. 12 hours seemed like two lifetimes ago. So much had happened between then and now. Now that she had seen Craig was in no immediate danger and now that she was sitting, exhaustion overtook her. Hunger raged a quick second. When was the last time she had eaten anything? Or drank anything?

She started to tell how she had headed up the mountain and her conversation with the Captain. When she recounted exactly what she had said, the agent's eyes narrowed and he interrupted her.

"Wait, Craig hasn't been threatened lately," Hawk said.

Emma thought back. Why had she said that? Her thoughts were thick and slow. Her vision started to blur and she felt nauseous.

Her head pitched forward and she fell slowly out of her chair. She tried to stay upright but had no strength in her body at all.

Once on the ground, her vision cleared and her head swam less. Agent Kinkaid swore under his breath and was around the small desk in an instant. "Are you OK? What happened?"

"I haven't eaten or drank anything in 24 hours. I need some food and water."

"Are you sure that's it? Should I go get a doctor?"

"No, I'm fine," she said, pushing herself into a sitting position. "I just need something to drink especially. Some food would be good too though."

He jumped up and practically ran behind the desk. He came back out with a thermos and a bottle of water.

"Here," he said, kneeling down and thrusting them at her.

She uncapped the water and drank greedily. Her throat hurt as it went down but it was still the best water she had ever tasted. She opened the thermos and smelled. Heavenly. "Chicken noodle?"

He smiled, the first one she'd seen. It changed his face from hard and stern to pleasant, inviting. "Yep. My best friend made it. He's a fantastic cook."

Emma wondered if that was code for lover. Probably not, but could be. She poured some soup and sipped it. Her stomach woke up and demanded more. She tried not to slurp.

A thought struck her. "Wait, she said, looking at him. How did you know my name? And why is the FBI investigating this? Why not the local police?" Another question hit her in the gut. "And why was Craig wearing a bulletproof vest?"

Agent Kinkaid eyed her, smile gone, face not giving an inch.

He stood up and walked back behind the desk. "I understand that you have questions Miss Hill, but I need mine answered first. When you think you are ready," he said with an air of finality.

Emma pushed herself back up onto the chair. Her brain was working again.

"I guess I didn't start at the beginning before. The reason I thought that something criminal might have happened to Craig was my ex-husband said something that made me scared for him."

This time Emma started from the night before. She told how she had been leaving the Crystal Creek wildfire after fighting it all day. She had heard someone yell in the smoldering woods and went in to investigate. She had found the hunter with the broken leg, built a travois to carry him out, and almost pulled him completely out of the fire when a falling tree had knocked her head-first into a rock, knocking her out. Craig had found her, put her in a helicopter and promised to pick her up at 8 o'clock in the morning. For some reason this part embarrassed her but she pushed that aside.

She watched the agent's face closely as she told the story. Something was going on here and she wanted to find out what. Agent Kinkaid was a closed book, but when she told him how she had first seen Craig and thought for sure he was dead her eyes teared up. She could have sworn the agent's did too. Stranger and stranger.

He asked many questions about the forest and the clearing and the building and even exactly how Craig was laying on the ground. Occasionally he made a notation on his pad.

When she got to the part where she put him in the helicopter she stopped talking.

"So what happened to your arm?" he said, motioning to her bandage.

"That happened after I left the scene. My day just got worse and worse."

"Tell me. Even if you don't think it's related it could be."

The car! Thinking about getting pulled over made her realize the hospital's car was still sitting on the side of the road. Maybe Jerry would go get it for her.

When she shared how she had been pulled over Agent Kinkaid's jaw clamped down in what looked like anger. He sat up straighter in his chair, leaning forward and peering into her soul again. Emma started to feel nervous. She wasn't sure where this was going.

"What was the officer's name?"

"Jeffries."

A look of recognition crossed his face. He muttered something under his breath. Emma thought it was "Bastard".

"What were you arrested for?"

"I still don't know, he never told me."

"Where are the papers you signed when you left?"

"Uh, I think I left the manila envelope in the ambulance with Jerry."

"Call him and ask him to bring them

here," he said, leaning over the desk to hand her a cell phone.

Emma did. Jerry said he would be by as soon as he could.

He motioned for her to go on.

When she finished telling the part about the woman who had sliced her he asked for a complete physical description of her. Emma struggled to remember every detail. When she recounted a mole she had remembered on her face the Agent nodded in recognition again.

"You got lucky there. You were probably meant to get a much worse lesson than that cut on your arm." When he said the word lesson he mimed quotation marks in the air.

Realization hit Emma like a load of bricks. "Are you saying that someone put her up to it?"

"Yes, I am. Look Miss Hill, you need to know what you are dealing with here so you can protect yourself. Can I trust you to keep quiet about something and not even tell your friend Jerry?"

Emma nodded, struck silent with fear.

"Good, because this is important. If you can't keep quiet, more lives may be in jeopardy because of it. I am investigating corruption in the Westwood Harbor police department. Your ex-husband, Norman Foster, and his friend, Peter Jeffries, are both very high on my list of dirty cops. Jeffries prefers to use other criminals to do his dirty work. This is not the first time I have come across a story like this. The last person lost part of her ear and has a very big scar on her face. She missed losing an eyeball by about a half an inch.

Emma's hand crept to her right ear, then just under her eye. Horror filled her.

"Now finish your story and then I will find you a place to stay tonight."

Chapter 6

Norman entered the station high on life. He couldn't wait to hear the day's events. He'd had a few calls on his cell phone while he was *busy* but he chose to ignore them. He preferred to get his news the old fashioned way so he could see the emotions on people's faces firsthand. Fear was his favorite emotion to see. Incredulity, his second. Both made him feel powerful, and very much in control.

He took the elevator straight up to his office. No one that he passed greeted him or looked at him. Most of the lower ranking officers were scared of him but a few were on his payroll. Many of the sergeants and above hated him and how he did business, but some tolerated him because they recognized him as one of their kind. Funny thing about being a cop - not many could retire after 20 years of service the same person they were when they were hired. The least affected had become bitter, hard. 20 years of dealing with people who spit on you and tried to stab you and bite you would do that to anyone. The most affected had become criminals themselves and just didn't know it. And then there were cops like Norman. Cops who got into police work because of the power and authority it wielded. Cops who started out shrewd and conniving. Cops who knew very well where the line is between cop and criminal, but think that criminal-in-a-cop-suit is more fun.

Norman's thoughts were cool and calm, like his demeanor. After his romp with Chloe and Lydia he had showered, shaved again, and put on freshly pressed slacks and a polo shirt. He spent little time on his dark hair, he didn't need to; it tamed itself. He felt relaxed and ready to put on a show of shock at the news of a dead firefighter and an arrested ex-wife. Of course she wasn't arrested for the big crime yet. He had only started to fuck with her. When he was done with her she'd be begging to take him back, because he could protect her. And he would protect her. He'd get her out of jail with a little help from more planted evidence and Senator Oberlin, but only after he'd completely broken her mentally.

He practically rubbed his hands together at the thought, but stopped himself. He had a reputation to protect.

On his desk was a note from Jeffries. *I need to see you now! Find me.* Norman frowned. That sounded like bad news. He went down to the Receiving Desk to look for Jeffries and nose around a little.

Sergeant Daly was at the desk. "Where's Jeffries?" Norman growled.

"Doing paperwork somewhere. Check out back," came the reply.

"Anything going on today?"

"Nah, nothing major."

Norman's eyebrows raised imperceptibly. Nothing major?

"What's going on with the Crystal Creek fire?" he prodded.

"Nothing, I think it's almost out."

Norman grunted. Nothing? This sergeant would know if any of his officers had been sent up for a missing person or a dead person. Where they still conducting the search on their own? Most of the day was gone.

He left the room, looking for Jeffries. He found him in his car parked behind the station.

Jeffries saw him coming and shook his head. Norman's pace quickened. *Just what in the fuck did that mean?*

"I managed to fingerprint her but then I sent Cassandra in to fuck with her and she got sliced up on her arm. The Sergeant made me release her to the medics."

"Who the fuck told you to sic Cassandra on her?" Norman's face was red. He felt like the top of his head was going to pop right off.

"I just thought it would be good for her. Scare her a little more," Jeffries practically whined.

"Did you happen to tell Cassandra *not* to slice her up?" Norman demanded.

Jeffries looked down. Norman knew he had his answer. Jeffries was a fucking idiot who couldn't be trusted not to fuck shit up. "Fuck you dumbass. Now I gotta fix it!"

Norman stomped back into the station. He thought about it. True, she wasn't here anymore, but she had been processed and she had been terrorized. This really wasn't too big of a deal, he could work with it. Now to figure out what was going on with the missing firefighter. He walked back to the receiving desk to talk to

Sergeant Daly.

"Hey this morning I heard the firefighters calling up a helicopter to search for a missing fireman. Did they find him?"

"Oh yeah, they found him, but he must have been hurt. He was flown to the hospital."

Norman's jaw twitched. The hospital? "Is there an investigation?"

"Nah, they never called us."

Norman grunted again and turned on his heel, heading to his office. Masterson was flown to the hospital, but no one called the cops for an investigation? Was he alive? And if he was alive had no one figured out he was shot yet? Was he alive but so burnt no one could see the bullet wounds?

Norman's hand shook as he pressed the elevator button. Luckily he was alone. He stared at his hand, willing it to steady. Panic and fear were not emotions Norman allowed himself to feel. He had learned to slam a lid on any feeling that betrayed his sense of control a long time ago.

He learned that at the hand of his mother. Norman never knew his father, if indeed he even had one. Norman's mother had been just mean enough and just crazy enough to make a deal with the devil, or maybe even have sex with the devil. Norman could never imagine a normal man wanting to impregnate his mother. She had been tall, and strong like a man. Her hair had been cropped short so she didn't have to brush it, she said. She had hated life, and every person on the earth, including Norman. She started beating him with a horse whip when he was little. He never had a memory of not being hit at least once each day by that thing.

By the time he was 13 though, he was big enough to take it away from her and she stopped. Her mental abuse had not stopped though. By this time she had been an alcoholic for over 15 years and her liver was starting to give out. Her stomach distended and her skin had started to darken in places. The more miserable she became, the more she tried to kill herself with a bottle, or goad Norman into doing it for her. Sometimes she would raise her hand like she was going to hit him and then laugh when he flinched. "Little baby boy," she would mock. "Are you going to wee-wee in your pants baby? Is the baby-diddums scared of the big bad lady?" Norman learned very well to not give an inch of emotion. He also learned to hate.

Norman entered his office and tore himself away from his thoughts. He called the hospital and asked what room Craig Masterson was in. "I don't have that information sir," the female voice on the other end said.

"Is he a patient?"

"A Craig Masterson was admitted this morning, sir, but there is no record of what room or floor he was admitted to and no record of him being released.

"Is he dead?" Norman demanded.

"Dead? Why, I don't know sir, but there is no record of him, uh, dying."

Norman slammed the phone down. This was not helpful. He needed to talk to someone in the hospital. He had a couple of contacts there - a security guard in the E.R. who was on the payroll but didn't have much access to the computers. A doctor in the geriatric ward caught with cocaine, but Norman had let him go as long as he remembered the 'favor'. A cook in the cafeteria who Norman had sent to jail for marijuana possession, but Norman had not reported the meth lab in his basement, so the cook owed him a favor too.

Norman looked in his rolodex for the doctor's number. A few minutes later he had tracked down Doctor Paloma and was on hold waiting for him to find something out. Inwardly Norman fumed. Outwardly he sat relaxed in his office chair.

A click on the line told him Dr. Paloma was back. "Yeah, Craig Masterson was admitted this morning and went straight to surgery. He's in the ICU now, room 1214, but his room is being guarded.

"Guarded? By who?" Norman bit the inside of his lip, hard, willing his face to remain impassive. He thought he probably knew the answer to that question.

"Two FBI agents."

Norman sat for a second. So that's why no one had called them. The FBI had taken over the case even before the police had known there was one. What a fuckup. But why was he alive? And how had they heard so quickly?

"One more question doctor, and then you can get back to your evening. What is his condition?"

"Well, um, I'm not trying to make a joke here, but he is listed as guarded. And that's all I know. There are no records in the computer yet, and the nurse said that the doctor hasn't let anyone see the chart."

"How bad is guarded?"

"That means he is being watched closely as his condition could go either way."

"Got it doc. I'll be talking to you."

Norman replaced the receiver quietly. In his mind, he picked the heavy phone up and threw it across the office. In his mind, when officer Franks looked up at the noise from his desk in the big room beyond, Norman grabbed the phone and smashed Franks' face in with it until shards of bone littered the floor.

Norman bit his cheek harder and willed himself to calm down. So Masterson was alive, and could be talking. But even he didn't know who shot him, so all wasn't lost yet. Hell, maybe the FBI would still be fooled by the planted gun at the scene and the letters in Masterson's car, if they found them.

Norman just needed to do a little damage control, that was all. He needed some time to think about this.

He grabbed his keys and headed out to do some thinking.

***

Norman ended up at the Black Dog Saloon. He was wound up tight, and he'd never be able to think of what to do unless he could work off some of this stress first.

He pulled open one of the big red doors and pushed past the bouncer standing inside. The bouncer made a move to stop him, but held back when he saw who Norman was. *Smart move asshole, probably the smartest thing you've done all week.* Norman thought.

Norman went up to the bar and ordered a tequila shot. He looked around lazily. There were always good prospects at any bar, but he didn't just want a good prospect. He wanted a great one. He never knew exactly what he was looking for, but he knew he would know it when he saw it.

The bar was dark but not crowded. There were maybe 12 people at the bar, and 30 people at tables, with a few on the dance floor.

There.

Standing by a booth, talking to the women sitting down. He was tall, taller than Norman, but older. Probably 15 years older, dressed in a typical bar outfit, jeans and black leather biker vest over a black t-shirt. He looked tough and mean and strong, but was beginning to get a bit of a beer belly. Norman noticed he had one slim scar hooking down his left cheek. *Matching scars, coming up.*

Norman headed to the bathroom, and purposely tripped over the man's feet as he went. The man snarled, "Watch it buddy!" Norman looked him dead in the eyes and waited a beat. The man fell silent, unsure. Norman continued on. As he pushed the bathroom door open he heard the group of women break out into tinkling laughter. Norman smiled, a flat, evil, deadly smile.

In the bathroom, he checked his pockets and holsters. Everything was in order.

He sidled back out towards the man, breath under control, emotions in check.

The man was leaning over the table now, in deep conversation with one of the women.

Norman glided up to him without making a sound, eyes on the man, peripheral vision noticing the women who could see him fall silent. One looked scared, eyes wide. The other looked excited, with a small smile playing on her lips. He might try to talk to her later.

He shoved the man in the shoulder, hard. "What did you say about me?"

The man stood up. His vest had several patches and emblems on it. The only one Norman bothered to read was one that looked like a name: Saint.

'Saint' eyed Norman up and down, looking for a weakness. Norman saw irritation and anger in his face, but no fear. *Good, this guy will be fun.*

Saint looked indecisive, like he didn't want to fight, but he knew he had to or he could kiss talking to these ladies goodbye. He planted a snarl on his face. "I said I hoped you could find your own ass when you got in there."

A ghost of Norman's deadly smile reappeared. "That's what I thought you said." His right hand shot out in a testing jab towards Saint's soft-looking gut. Saint was ready for it. He didn't even grunt. He just took it. Saint's gut might have a bit of a beer belly growing on top of it, but the hard sheet of muscle was totally intact.

The bar hadn't noticed yet, although Norman was positive the bouncers had been watching him since he walked in. They noticed, they knew, he was sure.

Saint smiled his own deadly smile. "That all you got?" He kicked his right leg back into a fighting stance and put his hands up. With his left he motioned 'come on' to Norman.

Norman assumed his own fighting stance. This guy knew how to fight. Norman would see what he had and then pull out his backups if he needed to. For the first time since he walked into the police station his agitations were truly gone. All that existed was this man, this bar, this beating, and the soup of adrenaline and cortisol rushing through his veins. Fighting worked way better than sex.

The bar had noticed now. The music was still playing but people were yelling and starting to circle them. The bouncers hovered outside the circle, ready to break up any side fights or pull off anyone who decided to help Saint. They knew the drill when Norman walked in. It always ended in a fight, and if they pulled Norman off anyone or didn't pull friends off Norman, one of them was getting arrested for something they may or may not have done. Norman was a smart bastard who kept his ear to the ground and kept files on everyone.

Norman threw the first punch. A high hook to the right. Saint blocked it and countered to Norman's jaw. Norman pulled back but was grazed. Damn, this man was probably professionally trained. That was probably good though, Norman liked to fight dirty. Usually the guys who were boxers just boxed.

They circled for a second without much room. Norman stepped inside quickly and went for an eye with an open, rigid hand. Saint bobbed then danced away and chuckled a little. Norman thought he heard Saint mutter 'baby move' under his breath. He would pay for that.

Norman stopped advancing and stood there. "So I underestimated you. What say we just forget this thing?"

Saint relaxed a little and laughed again. "Sure fella, whatever you say."

Norman dropped his guard and put his hand out. Saint ignored it, watching him. *Fucker.* Now Norman was getting pissed. This guy was too quick but Norman was itching to get in there and land some blows. Saint would just side-step him if he rushed him. He needed to get Saint angry and on the offensive.

"Nothing to see here folks, break it up," he told the crowd, who backed up. The bouncers warily exchanged glances but stayed put. Norman pulled over a chair and sat down next to the booth where Saint had been talking to the women. He tipped a wink to the woman who had looked excited before. She was in her 30s, long brown hair, and too much makeup wearing a tight black bustier that practically spilled her boobs out the top. "So what was so interesting about that pussy?" he asked her loudly.

The three other women at the booth eyed

him warily, but the one he winked at giggled merrily. She loved this kind of shit. He was glad she didn't seem to have any attraction to Saint or Norman probably would have felt her jump on his back and hit him with a beer bottle.

He watched Saint out of the corner of his eye - he was standing where Norman had left him, probably trying to decided if he really wanted to fight or not. Norman had no doubt that Saint could kick his ass in an honest fight, but Norman wouldn't fight honestly and Saint probably knew it.

Saint walked over to the bar and ordered a beer. Norman had to shift in his seat to see him. When he sat down on the bar stool Norman stood up and rushed him, landing a hard hit to the temple. Saint fell off the seat onto the floor. Norman jumped on top of him and hit blow after blow, head, nose, chin. Blood spouted out of Saint's nose and soaked everything, making Norman's fists slide against Saint's face. Hands grabbed Norman from behind and hauled him up.

"That was dirty fightin'" a huge biker yelled in his face. The smell of stale beer and bad breath assaulted Norman. "You get the hell out of here!"

Norman snuck a hand in his pocket and brought the hand out with his brass knuckle duster on his middle finger. He grabbed the biker by the shirt and pounded him hard to the temple. The biker's face sliced open from eye to ear and a flap of skin dangled down an inch. A woman screamed behind them and the crowd pressed in again. Norman shoved the biker backwards and whirled around towards Saint. Saint had stood up and was eying the hand with the knuckle duster warily, sneaking glances at the bouncers for help, blood running down his face and soaking his shirt. He grabbed a beer bottle off the counter and waited for Norman to come again.

Norman stood up straight, grinning. He knew exactly what he was going to do about that fucker Masterson. He headed for the bar exit past everyone backpedaling to get out of his way.

Chapter 7

Emma couldn't believe her luck. Agent Kinkaid said he wanted her safe, but he couldn't spare any manpower so he was going to get her a cot and talk the doctors into letting her sleep in Craig's room. Ordinarily overnight visitors were never allowed in the ICU. He also said he was going to try to get her a look at Craig's chart.

She had stolen a second away with Jerry to ask him to go get the car and he had said sure. He also said he would go to her house and get her a bag with some shower items and some clothes. She really owed him dinner or three dinners or something when this was all over. He had said he had news too but he would wait to share it until things were calmer. She hadn't even bugged him. She could only think of herself and Craig right now. She hoped that didn't make her a bad friend.

When she walked back up to Craig's room, she got a much different reception from the two men there this time. They smiled and introduced themselves. Their names were Adrian and Bret. She already forgot who was who but she tried not to beat herself up. She was surprised she could remember her own name at the moment.

She pushed open the door to Craig's room and peeked inside. A nurse stood over the bed, bandage in hand.

"Hi," Emma said. She had seen this nurse

before in the E.R. a few times. Her name tag said Katy, with a big yellow smiley sticker on it.

"Hi," the nurse said back and busied herself with the bandage on Craig's face.

"So you are going to sleep here tonight? That's unusual," Katy said while she worked.

Emma eased into the room and sank onto the small cot on the other side of the bed, pushed into the corner. "I know. I can't believe they are going to let me."

"Me neither," Katy said sharply.

Emma wasn't sure what that meant so she just kept quiet.

Emma laid down and closed her eyes, just for a second, boots and uniform still on. She kept her mind busy trying to make some sense out of the day and everything she had learned. Norman was being investigated by the FBI? She never had gotten any answers to her questions to Agent Kinkaid either. How did he know her name? Why had Craig been wearing a bulletproof vest? And the FBI? Thinking about it, she was so glad it was the FBI investigating this, and not the local cops, but why, how had that happened?

Emma's questions drifted through her mind slowly. They took on a lyrical quality, lulling her deeper and deeper. She fell asleep within 2 minutes, worn out from head to toe.

Dimly, some part of her was aware when people entered or exited the room. Nurses came and went. She overheard a conversation between a doctor and a nurse about reducing medication. The sun rose. Jerry brought a bag in the room, then took her boots off and covered her with a blanket. More nurses. The sun set again. Agent Kinkaid came into the room and slipped a folder under her cot. A nurse came in to check on Craig but also grasped her wrist and checked her pulse. *I'm fine, just tired,* Emma tried to send to her telepathically.

At 4:15 a.m., the time she normally would have been rising for work, she woke, alert and full of questions. She looked around the dark room and tried to gauge how much of what she thought had happened really had, and what was a dream. Had she really slept for about 28 hours straight? Here was her bag, and the blanket. Here was the folder. She looked at Craig. No change. Her neck was stiff and her lower back a little sore. Her stomach was completely empty and her bladder totally full. She needed some water fast, and then a bathroom. She looked around, not wanting to leave the room just yet.

She checked the bag Jerry had brought her and sure enough, there were two water bottles and some energy bars from her pantry with her clothes. Emma drank both the water bottles empty first, and then shoved both of the energy bars in her mouth, barely stopping to chew. As she ate she prodded the bandage on her arm, trying to assess how well the cut was healing without actually seeing it. Everything seemed to be OK.

She got up and crossed to Craig. The bandage still covered much of his face and he still had the tube down his throat, breathing for him. His skin color was good though; She thought he looked much better than before she fell asleep. She smoothed his hair down and whispered in his ear "Hi Sweetie, I'm here. I'm going to leave the room for 20 minutes, but I'll be back."

She went back to the cot and grabbed her bag, shoving the file that Agent Kinkaid had brought her into it. She headed to the door, opened it an inch and peeked out. She was happy to see two FBI agents still outside the room. One was asleep in the chair and one was standing, probably trying hard to stay awake. Oh, that was Officer Kinkaid sleeping, she noticed. She wondered if he was pulling 24 hour duty here. Now that her mind was rested and sharp again she started to think about how strange he seemed during their interview, like he was emotionally involved in this case.

She didn't recognize the other agent. She pushed the door open far enough that she could tiptoe out of it. He snapped his head around to look at her. "Hi," she whispered. "If I go use the bathroom will you let me back in?"

"Yes, bosses orders you are allowed in the room," he said, his voice pitched low.

Phew. Emma headed to the bathroom, changed her clothes to jeans and a dark blue pullover, plus comfy sneakers, then washed up in the sink the best she could. She left the bathroom intending to find some more food. Agent Kinkaid was waiting outside for her.

He smiled faintly. "Sleeping Beauty is awake."

"Yeah, what was that about? Did I miss anything?"

His smile widened and he almost seemed about to laugh. But then the smile fell away. "You had a rough day. I'm not surprised you slept so long. And no, you didn't miss anything. Are you going to find some food?"

She nodded.

"Mind if I tag along?"

"Please," she said, heading for the elevator.

They went down to the cafeteria, Emma grabbing fruit and pastries plus three little cartons of milk. She would have loved to have bacon and eggs but the grill didn't open till 6, a sign said. Agent Kinkaid got some coffee. They paid and sat down at a table.

"Did you read through his chart yet? I was hoping you would interpret it for me. The doctor and I keep playing phone tag and the nurses just say 'you have to talk to the doctor.'"

Emma looked at him inquisitively. "Is that what's in the folder?"

He nodded.

She opened her bag and pulled it out. "I'll do it right now."

She opened the chart, flipping to the back to read it from the beginning. It started with the notes in the E.R., a few scribbled lines about where and how he was found. He was typed and crossmatched immediately and had a wide open flow of donor blood within 10 minutes. X-ray found no spinal issues but did find one bullet lodged in his cheek. It had smashed a molar on the way there.

Emma's hands flew to her mouth. She'd

personally seen several gunshot victims and even watched a few die in front of her, but she hadn't loved any of them. This was much harder.

The chart noted he was wearing a bullet proof vest with a bullet in the back of it. They had removed the vest and found his back black and blue from the impact.

A physical exam found a bullet wound in the back of his neck. This bullet traveled through his neck to his skull, around the skull, and into his cheek, lodging there. There were many more small wounds in the back of his head. Examination of his helmet found a bullet had shattered the back of it, but not penetrated all the way through. The part of the helmet facing his skull was battered and bulging, causing these small plastic shrapnel wounds.

Three bullets. He'd been shot once in the back and twice in the back of the head. Emma felt sick. If he hadn't been wearing that bulletproof vest he'd be dead.

She relayed all of this to Agent Kinkaid. He nodded. He knew this part.

"Agent Kinkaid, do you know why he was wearing a bulletproof vest?" Emma asked slowly, emotion still clogging her throat, one tear winding its way down her cheek.

He reached out and took her hand and nodded. "I do, and I'll tell you why when you are done reading the chart," he said softly. "And call me Hawk."

Emma looked in his eyes and knew something had changed in the last 28 hours while she'd been asleep. He trusted her now, or wanted to treat her like a friend. Something. "Hawk." She tried it out, then nodded.

He let go of her hand and she turned the page. Craig had been rushed straight to surgery. The bullet in his cheek had been removed, the smashed molar had been pulled, and his neck had been opened up to see what else was damaged in that sensitive area. His skull was grooved, but fully intact. The bullet had entered incredibly close to his spine, and the swelling in the back of his neck was extreme. His jugular vein had been nicked, but his jugular artery, not touched. Emma's eyes flew over the surgery notes. She couldn't believe how lucky he'd been. Everything had been fixed. A full recovery was expected.

So why was he still unconscious?

Emma turned the page. The surgeon had recommended a medically induced coma for 48 hours to let the swelling go down in his neck before he started moving around. There had been a bit of swelling on the brain too because of the groove in his skull, and the surgeon was afraid the pressure in his head would cause him to thrash and permanently injure his neck if they had let him wake before that.

Emma skimmed through the last 24 hours of notes. Great vital signs. All positive indications of healing. Signs of the swelling going down. His medication would be reduced starting at 6 o'clock this morning and he could wake as early as 10! Relief flooded her. She was going to get him back. He was going to be ok.

"Hawk, they're going to wake him up

today!" She stood up and grabbed her stuff, intending to run all the way back to the ICU.

"Wait, wait, Emma. What time?"

She stopped and looked at the clock on the wall. "Well, they are going to start reducing his meds in about an hour."

"OK, so we have time. Sit, tell me what else the chart said."

"It says he's going to be fine. The bullet hit a big vein and touched his skull but didn't shatter it. His spine was bruised too, but should be fine. That's why he's been unconscious. They've kept him under with drugs so the swelling in his spine could go down."

"He's going to recover then?" Hawk's face was tight and guarded.

"A full recovery is expected. Everything was fixed in surgery."

Hawk's face was unreadable for a moment. His eyes looked dead and dull. Emma couldn't tell if he was upset, or struggling with something. Her eyebrows creased together. "Hawk?"

He crumpled. His hand covered his eyes and he took a deep, shaky breath like he was trying not to cry. Emma knew right then why Craig had been wearing a bullet proof vest and how the FBI knew about Craig being hurt so quickly. She gave Hawk a few minutes to recover his control before continuing. "Hawk, I know you are running this show, but I think it's time you tell me what's really going on here."

Hawk wiped his eyes and gave her that faint smile again. "I'm going to Emma. But you have to promise me one thing. That you won't think any differently of Craig when you hear it."

Chapter 8

Emma couldn't find any saliva in her mouth. She licked her lips but it was like sandpaper sliding over a cracked windshield. The white cafeteria walls pressed in on her. *Not feel any different about Craig?* Her mind flew to the worst scenarios. *He was married. He was gay. He was living a double life.* But none of those explained why he would be wearing a bulletproof vest. *He's a cop.*

Her heart dropped. No matter what Hawk ended up saying here, the truth would reveal that Craig had lied to her about something. That much was obvious.

"I can't promise I won't feel different," she finally squeaked out.

Hawk looked worried. "Well can you promise to keep an open mind?"

"Yes, I can do that."

Hawk leaned forward and kept his voice low. "Emma, Craig is an FBI agent, and my best friend. In fact, he was almost my brother-in-law until his fiance, my sister, was killed three years ago - probably by your ex-husband. That's why he was wearing a bulletproof vest. He always wears it under his t-shirt. That's why he was wearing a bulletproof helmet too, I ordered that for him myself."

Emma's world swam. FBI. Fiance.

Norman. Best friend. Killed. Her thoughts tumbled together. She looked down at the table, trying to process everything she had just heard. It was no use. She couldn't make sense of it. She didn't want to make sense of it. After the hell she had been through over the last few days, her tortured mind had started to hope again that when Craig recovered maybe they could make a life together. Maybe they would get married and start a family. Maybe her life could settle down into a sweet rhythm. But now, that fantasy was shattered. Craig was FBI. Not a firefighter at all. Norman had killed someone. Norman had killed Craig's fiance. Norman had killed Hawk's sister. Norman had killed a woman.

"Look, Emma, I know this is a lot to take in all at once. Craig would not have lied to you if he didn't have to. He is undercover, working for me. We have several agents undercover in departments around the city, all working on the same case. He was required to lie to you. But he likes you a lot. I think he is starting to feel more for you than just like actually. He thinks you are really special and he talks about you all the time. He was very concerned how you would take it when you discovered he was FBI."

This news did nothing to help Emma's outlook. There was so much more to this than the relationship between Emma and Craig. Emma looked at Hawk again. *My ex-husband killed your sister? If Norman already killed someone then did he try to kill Craig too?*

"Hawk, who do you think shot Craig?"

Hawk looked over at the cafeteria workers

who had started to open up more of the kitchen. He seemed to be deciding what to say here.

He looked back at Emma, determination on his face. "Someone wants us to think *you* did."

Emma's mouth dropped open. Her swirling thoughts fled in alarm. "Me!" She pushed back in her chair, looking desperately around the room. Was she about to be arrested again?

Hawk put a hand out. "Calm down Emma, I know you didn't shoot Craig. But someone planted some evidence to try to make it look like you did."

Emma couldn't believe what she was hearing. She felt like she was in a bad movie. On top of everything that had already happened to her now she was being framed for attempted murder too?

"What-What kind of evidence?"

"We found the gun in the woods, partially buried, that probably was used to shoot Craig. Ballistics tests are being done right now to see for sure, but I'm confident they will come back positive. The only fingerprints on the gun belong to you."

Emma got up and paced back and forth in front of the table. Her fingernails bit into her palms. She didn't even own a gun, so how could her fingerprints get on a gun? *Wait!* She remembered just getting fingerprinted the day before yesterday. She turned on her heel and slid back into the chair, balled up fists on the table. "How do you have my fingerprints?" she demanded.

"We have access to them from when you were in the Army."

"Oh." She felt deflated a little bit.

"Are you wondering if the local police would have had access to them?"

She nodded fiercely.

"No, they wouldn't normally have been able to search that database. They can request it if they have a reason to, and the Army would normally cooperate."

"I was fingerprinted the day before yesterday when I was arrested."

Hawk nodded. "Yes, I know. In fact, I'm pretty sure your ex-husband was behind your arrest. As I told you before, he and Jeffries are both dirty, and I believe they work together a lot."

Emma looked down again, chewing on her lip. She looked back up at Hawk. "I'm sorry about your sister."

Hawk smiled. "Thank you. I am too. She was a wonderful, sweet woman. And someday Norman will pay for what he did to her."

Emma nodded and glanced at the clock. "I still need to talk to you more, a lot more, but it's almost 6. They are going to lower Craig's medication soon."

Hawk nodded. "Let's get upstairs."
***

Back in the room, Emma sat next to Craig's bed in the chair and held his hand. Hawk stood at the foot of the bed and they continued their conversation, quietly, alert for interruptions. When the nurse came in to change his medication level, they both watched in silence.

Nothing changed. Craig slept peacefully, no sign of the dimples Emma loved so much. Emma studied his face, trying to figure out how she felt about him being an FBI agent.

She was conflicted. She had sworn she would never date another cop a long time ago. But was he really a cop like Norman was a cop? And he certainly was not one of the bad guys. She remembered something he had said to her an eternity ago: "I try very hard every day to be one of the good guys." She could believe that. He was a good guy from his head to his toes.

And the fact that he had lied to her? That part was a bit easier to forget for her. She had lied to him too, at least by omission, and he had forgiven her. Plus he had to lie, he didn't have a choice.

She thought back to her mistakes in the relationship. When she had gotten hurt at work a few weeks ago and had the vision of the perfect man for her while unconscious, the man she was convinced couldn't be Craig, which was horrible because Craig actually did seem to be perfect for her. Then she'd gone and dated that scumbag doctor while she was also dating Craig, because his darker hair and darker skin meant he could be the man from the vision. Then she'd asked out one of Craig's friends practically right in front of Craig because she thought he could have been the man from the vision. That had hurt Craig badly, and he'd walked out of her life, almost for good. He had read her letter of explanation though, and although it hadn't been enough to make him forgive her, the night that he had found her unconscious in the woods his heart had let go of the hurt instantly.

Thinking about that night clinched it for her. Her mind discovered what her heart already knew. She loved Craig the firefighter, and she loved Craig the FBI agent too. Her heart swelled with it. Her soul ached with it.

Come on baby, wake up please. I want to squeeze your hand and feel you squeeze mine back. I want to see you smile and laugh and hear your voice. I want to see those luscious dimples light up your face.

The door opened again. A neat, compact doctor came in. He looked from Hawk to Emma and said, "I'm glad you are both here. Mr. Masterson is going to wake up in a few hours, and we are going to have to ask both of you to leave."

"What? Why?" Hawk leaned toward the doctor intensely.

Because when he wakes there will be several staff members here. He will need to be watched closely and assessed for neurological deficiencies. There won't be room in here for you.

Hawk flicked his eyes at Emma, then back to the doctor. "I need to be in here doc. I'll stand in the corner. I won't say a word, and I won't take up any space. You won't even know I'm here."

The Doctor looked at Emma pointedly.

"I'll go, that's fine," she said, smoothing Craig's hair. She didn't want to go, but Hawk *needed* to be here for a few reasons, she was sure. She just *wanted* to be here.

"Fine Agent Kinkaid, but not one word," the doctor warned.

"You got it. What time will all this happen?"

"As soon as he shows signs of stirring. If there aren't any by 10 o'clock we will give him a drug that will counteract the one that's been keeping him under."

Emma leaned over and kissed Craig on the cheek, then whispered in his ear, "I'll be close by baby, I'll come back to see you as soon as I can."

She gathered her stuff together and put it by the door, ready to go, then she resumed her place at Craig's side. She eyed the phone, wondering if she should call Jerry and see if he could have lunch. She could use something to take her mind off not being in the room as Craig woke up.

The doctor examined Craig, pronounced him good, and left the room.

"Sorry," Hawk said.

"That's OK, I'm just glad they are letting you stay."

"Me too. I would have put up a fight though. Are you going to stay in the hospital?"

"Yes, I had planned on it. Maybe I will just go and have lunch."

Hawk nodded. "Do me a favor? If you see Norman or Jeffries, or any cops at all really, come back up here and sit with the guards outside the door, ok?"

Emma nodded. "Do you think I'll see them?"

Hawk sighed, pushing a big hand through his military hair cut. "I don't know what they have planned. I expect Norman to be pretty desperate when he finds out Craig is alive. I expect he also would rather you were still sitting in the cellblock too. Your friend did you a big favor when he got you out of there."

Emma shivered at the thought of still sitting in the cellblock, alone, scared, and having no idea what was going on with Craig. *Thank God for Jerry getting me out of there and thank God for Hawk, letting me stay here,* she thought with appreciation.

Emma's trained ears picked up an increase in the speed of Craig's heartbeat on the monitor. Beep, beep, beep. She looked down at Craig and saw his eyelids flutter for a second. She grabbed his hand and squeezed it.

"Is he waking up?" Hawk asked, excitement in his voice.

Emma studied Craig's face, but it remained smooth, relaxed. "Not yet. But his heart rate is up. A nurse will probably be sent in here to stay soon, because when he starts breathing on his own he might fight this tube. They'll take it out at the first signs of that."

Still holding Craig's hand, she made a grab for the phone on the little table just out of her reach. Hawk fished something out of his pocket and gave her a cell phone. "Here, take this. It's Craig's, it's all charged up."

She smiled her thanks at him and dialed Jerry's number.

"Sure Em, I can meet you for lunch - I have to leave at 11:30 though."

***

On the way down to the cafeteria, Emma called work. She knew she had been put on the injured list when she got med-evaced down to the hospital, but she hadn't talked to anyone since. Fielding, the day supervisor answered. Emma was happy to get him; He was a super nice guy.

"Hi Fielding, it's Emma Hill, uh, I was injured a few days ago and just wanted to make sure I got taken off the schedule."

"Hi Emma, yeah, um, let me look at this note." He didn't sound happy to hear from her. Emma's brow creased.

He came back on. "How are you feeling anyway?"

"Pretty good. I haven't had any complications or anything."

"Yeah well, Emma, it says here that you've been suspended."

"Suspended!" A blood vessel beat at Emma's temple, marking time with her pounding heart. She had never been in trouble at work before.

"Yeah, well, it says that you got arrested?"

Emma put a hand over her eyes. How did work know about that already?

"Yeah, does it say that the cop who arrested me did it with no cause whatsoever and then he tried to get me killed?" Emma demanded, yelling.

"What, Emma slow down? What are you talking about?"

Forget it Fielding, it's not your fault. How long am I suspended for?"

"It says pending investigation."

"Ok thanks. Bye." Emma pushed the end call button viciously and strode faster down the hall. Suspended! Well fine, now she didn't have to worry about work for a while. She was going to turn this into a positive if it killed her. Craig was waking up today and she wasn't going to let anything ruin that.

Emma turned left into the cafeteria and tried to slow her breathing and take deeper breaths. No use staying upset over this. She had some money squirreled away to live on. Hawk would help her clear her name with the department. This would all get taken care of.

She walked around the perimeter of the room looking for Jerry.

She saw him, entering through the far entrance door, looking handsome in his khakis and pressed shirt. She'd never seen him wear anything but jeans before.

"Jerry," she called, waving her arm.

He smiled and walked to her, giving her a kiss on the cheek and then a bone-crushing hug.

"So how's Craig?" he asked.

"He's great. Showing signs of recovery. They are waking him up right now. They wouldn't let me stay in the room. That's why I called; I figured we could get some lunch and catch up." She almost told him she was suspended, but bit it back. She wanted to talk about more happy things right now - not bitch about work.

They each picked out some food from the cafeteria. Emma ravenous, got a turkey sandwich, fries, a big salad, some cottage cheese, a large coke, and a brownie for dessert.

Jerry laughed at her. "I never thought you'd out-eat me Em."

"I gotta eat now, while I have the chance. Who knows if I'll come back down for food once Craig is awake." She smiled at his ribbing. She had missed Jerry. She remembered something. "Jerry, you had news for me the other day? What was it?"

"Oh, yeah! I met someone!" His enthusiastic smile pulled Emma right in.

"You mean you met someone you really like? And not just one of your bed-buddies?" She asked incredulously. Jerry didn't seem to ever want to settle down, and he seemed to have an endless supply of women 'friends', most of whom had been in his bed at one time or another.

"Well, yeah, I do really like her, and I haven't even slept with her yet," he joked. "But honestly, it might be over before it really gets started." He was still smiling, so Emma wasn't sure if he was still joking or not.

"Over, why?"

"Well, she's too classy. I get all self-conscious around her. It's making me uncomfortable."

Emma was confused. "Too classy?"

"She's a theoretical physicist. An actual scientist! And a genius." He leaned forward, whispering. "And she's loaded. She drives a Jaguar."

Emma started working on her sandwich and mulled this over. She didn't know what to think of this information. She definitely didn't sound like Jerry's usual type. He tended towards hard-working, hard-drinking women, and never got serious with any of them. He always seemed out for just fun and he liked women that seemed out for the same thing.

He sat back, rubbing his bald head. "I don't know why she agreed to date me in the first place. I met her at the library - you know, the big one downtown. We had a call there but it turned out to be nothing. Some lady thought she swallowed a bee and she was allergic, but she never had a reaction. We sat around watching her and joking with her for 20 minutes, and then Beth went in the back to talk to her brother-in-law who works there. So I was just sitting there in the microfiche room waiting for Beth to come back and I couldn't keep my eyes off her. From the back she looked like my kind of woman, you know? And then when she came up to the desk we locked eyes and her eyes are the same color as yours Em. I've never seen anyone with eyes that light blue color other than you so I stared at her. I thought she was going to get offended but I still couldn't tear my eyes off her. Instead she smiled and then came over and talked to me."

Emma laughed. Typical Jerry, meeting women everywhere he went. His lean runner's body, paramedic uniform, and completely bald head apparently lured them in like flies to honey. Emma had seen it with her own eyes many times.

"I asked her out after my shift and she agreed. She's just in town doing research. We went out to lunch and she's really amazing and interesting, but I just keep feeling like I'm out of my league with her. I mean, I went out and bought these pants today so I wouldn't wear jeans again!"

Emma stopped eating long enough to lean forward and try to encourage Jerry. "Look Jerry, any woman would be lucky to have you, even a rich theoretical physicist. If you like her, then don't worry about it," she told him, trying to telegraph the same thing with her eyes.

Jerry sighed. "I know, that's what I keep telling myself."

Emma laughed around forkfuls of cottage cheese.

"She's actually going to meet me here at 11:30. That's why I have to go. We are going wine tasting."

"Wine tasting?" Emma had never seen Jerry drink wine. "At noon?"

"Yeah, I know right? Apparently that's the best time."

Jerry started to look around, watching for his new friend. "You tell me what you think of her when I call you later Em."

"OK Jerry, you know I will."

Jerry hopped up in his seat. "There she is!" He waved his arms. "Vivian, Vivian, over here!"

Emma craned her neck, very curious about this woman. Vivian smiled and waved back at Jerry, revealing a flash of white teeth. "She's gorgeous Jerry," Emma whispered.

"I know, way too gorgeous," Jerry whispered back.

She looked to be about Emma's height, with long, brown, wavy, hair held together in a loose clip over one shoulder. She had a perfect, light complexion and wide-set, large eyes. As she got closer, Emma was immediately struck by the sense of class and grace she exuded. Emma could see what Jerry was talking about right away. Everything about the woman said *money*. From her movie-star body to her perfectly shaped eyebrows plus her expensive silk scarf and black, leather knee-boots over dark slacks. Her makeup was simple though, and her only jewelry was small gem earrings in each ear.

She made it to the table and gave Jerry a small kiss on the cheek, then turned to Emma.

"Vivian, this is my best friend in the world and partner, Emma Hill. Emma this is Vivian Dashell."

Emma winced at the word partner, but shoved it out of her mind. She wanted to soak up impressions of Vivian to share with Jerry later. She smiled and held out her hand.

Vivian grasped it lightly, but didn't shake it. "Emma, dear, I've heard so much about you. I am so happy to finally meet you."

Emma was struck with how much Vivian's eyes did exactly copy her own unique shade of light blue. "Hi Vivian, it's nice to meet you too. Can you sit down?"

Vivian looked at Jerry, eyebrows raised. "We do have to go to get out to the winery by noon, but maybe we have a few minutes."

She sat down and smiled. "Emma, what are you doing here in the hospital? Are you working here today?"

"No, my, uh, boyfriend is in the ICU. He got hurt at work a few days ago."

"Oh no, that's horrible, is he going to be alright?" Vivian's eyebrows drew together in what seemed to be genuine concern. Emma liked her already.

"Yes, I think he is," She leaned back and sighed. "I really do think he'll be OK."

The phone Hawk had given her buzzed. Emma wasn't sure if she should answer it or not. She turned it over and a text message popped up on the screen. Emma couldn't help but read it. Hawk. *He's awake. The doctors are done. You can come back.*

"Oh, Jerry, Vivian, I'm so sorry but I have to go. Jerry, he's awake," she squeezed Jerry's arm too hard. "You guys have a great time." She rushed away from the table without waiting for them to respond, weaving between neighboring tables as fast as she could. She ran to the elevator and jammed the button a dozen times. "Hurry, hurry."

The elevator came and she filed in, not waiting for anyone else, but jamming the close doors button over and over. On the 12th floor she sprinted down the hall, past the agents at the door.

Pulling it open, she rushed into the room. Hawk was standing at the side of the bed in mid-sentence. He stopped talking and looked up at her. She barely registered the concerned look on his face and then looked at Craig. His eyes were open! He swung his head towards her, expression blank. She smiled and walked towards him. "Craig, you're awake, how do you feel?"

His eyebrows drew together like he was confused. He did not seem happy to see her. In a weak and raspy voice he asked Emma "What are you doing here?"

Hawk spoke up gently. "He doesn't remember anything from about the last week. Not even going to work the night before he was shot."

Emma pulled back like she was struck. Did that mean he didn't remember forgiving her?

Chapter 9

Emma felt like breaking down and crying right here. Or turning tail and running. Just hitting the trail and running out all this frustration and fear and anger. Frustration at having Craig stolen from her again. Fear that he'd never remember. Anger that this all had happened in the first place.

He didn't remember forgiving her. In fact, every time he looked at her he had that hurt look on his face, the one he wore right before he walked out of her house and out of her life.

She desperately wanted him to remember on his own. She couldn't imagine trying to explain to him that he had forgiven her. Because he had to feel the forgiveness himself. Explaining wouldn't do a damn thing.

Hawk excused them and took her out in the hall.

"The doctor called it retrograde amnesia and said he probably will remember the events that he has forgotten, but that he may not. He says the brain swelling may have caused it, or just the fact that his brain hadn't had the time to commit the short term memory into long term memory yet. As he heals more he may remember, or something may trigger the memories to return. He said we just have to wait and see."

Emma grabbed Hawk's hand and looked

imploringly up into his face. "Hawk, I did something stupid a week and a half ago and he was hurt by it, and mad at me. But he had forgiven me! When he put me into that helicopter he told me he wanted me to move in with him. He practically said he loved me. But now he doesn't remember it and he is upset with me again."

Hawk nodded along as she spoke, understanding filling his features. "Yes, I see that. I'm not sure what to do about it. Should we tell him, or just let him remember on his own?"

Emma dropped her head. "I don't know. It's torture for me to not be able to touch him and kiss him, but I can tell he doesn't even want me in the room! But just telling him he forgave me is not going to make him be able to feel it."

Hawk nodded again. "Why don't we just stay close, and fill him in on everything that's happened in the last few days and see what happens. We don't have to try to convince him to forgive you again, but maybe something will jog his memory."

"Ok," Emma whispered, hoping against hope that Hawk was right.

They went back in the room. Emma moved to the chair and Hawk brought in another chair from outside.

"Now that Emma's here we want to tell you what's been going on the last few days," he told Craig.

Craig nodded slowly, questioningly, eyebrows raised.

Hawk began, "So you already know you

were shot 2 days ago and you have been in a kind of medical coma ever since - think back - what is your last memory?"

Craig pondered. As if it hurt to do so, he closed his eyes and relaxed his head on the pillow. After a few moments he began to talk. "I remember talking to Frankie after an, ah, incident at the fire station. I remember Frankie telling me they were looking for volunteers for the wildfire and it would be a good idea if I volunteered, since I'd never been to one yet. I remember telling him I wanted to do it, and I remember driving home the next morning. I was scheduled to come up to the fire that evening for the night shift. And that's it. I don't remember getting home or anything after that."

Hawk and Emma exchanged a look. That was the day that he had come and found her in the woods.

"Ok, I'm going to tell you in a linear fashion everything that has happened since then." He nodded to Emma. "Emma, if I forget anything, interrupt me."

"Ok."

Hawk started talking, and Emma watched Craig closely for signs of recognition. When he told Craig that Emma had saved a hunter in the woods, only to be knocked over by a falling tree and then luckily found by Craig and med-evaced, there was a bit of a response. Craig looked at her wide-eyed and with more warmth. Hawk didn't share the part about Craig turning out to be the man in Emma's vision after all, or how Craig had acted like a man in love, because he didn't know it. Hawk then told Craig about Norman visiting Emma, Emma racing up the mountain to look for him, and how Emma found him. He shared how Emma had come back down the mountain and been arrested and attacked. Another wide-eyed look. Emma held up her bandaged arm.

Hawk backtracked here and detailed some things that Emma didn't know. That he had also become worried about Craig around 10, when he hadn't heard from him that morning. He didn't start looking for him till 11:00 though, when he was really worried. He called dispatch and was told that "There was no information available about the whereabouts of Mr. Masterson." This really worried him, since ordinarily they would just say "He's not working right now, or he's working right now." He called the hospital, but Craig hadn't been flown in yet. He headed up the mountain himself and spoke to Captain Lane himself. Captain Lane was similarly tight-lipped until he pulled out his FBI badge, effectively blowing his cover here in Westwood Harbor.

"Damn, Hawk, I'm sorry," Craig said, and hung his head.

Hawk laughed, "What are you sorry for? Sorry that some asshole shot you? Yeah, I'm sorry too. Don't be silly Craig, it's not your fault. Besides, my cover would have been blown soon anyway. Norman Foster is getting too dangerous. We are going to have to bring him in soon."

Craig looked confused again. "So, how much does Emma know?" He asked Hawk, sneaking a glance at Emma.

"Everything Craig, she knows you're FBI."

Craig sat up straighter in his bed and looked sideways at Emma. "How does she feel about it?" he said out loud, his eyes focused on her.

Emma wasn't sure if he was addressing her, or Hawk. A thrill raced up Emma's spine. *Does he care how I feel about him again?* She forgot to answer, locking her gaze on Craig's, everything else in the room falling away. She held tight to the chair with both hands, not wanting to run to him in case he wasn't sure yet, but wanting to run to him and cover the good side of his face with kisses. Wanting to jump right in that bed with him and indulge her every whim.

Hawk was silent for a moment, looking from Craig to Emma. "Um, well, I'm not sure but I think she's OK with it."

Emma couldn't read Craig's eyes, but she didn't care. She opened up her soul to him through her eyes. She gave him everything she had to give him. She laid herself bare and open and vulnerable. *I'm yours*, she thought. *If you'll just have me again.*

Craig gave her a crooked smile, one dimple showing up, then he tore his eyes back to Hawk.

Emma felt the heat of his stare leave her, and she sat back, disappointed.

"So, uh, where was I?" Hawk stammered, obviously feeling the fire himself and not sure what to do about it. "Oh yeah, so Captain Lane told me what happened and that you had just been found by Emma and just been sent out of there in a helicopter. She looked very grave when she told me and I feared the worst. I called in a team to cordon off the area and start a search and then I headed down to the hospital myself. No one here wanted to talk to me, because you were still in surgery. I finally found your doctor and put a guard on your surgery room who would follow you to this room. I talked to the hospital administration and got an empty office in the basement and started working out what I was going to do next. I got news that you were out of surgery so I came up to see you. Then I got news that a gun had been found at the scene to I went to fast-track the investigation on the gun."

"A gun at the scene?" Craig asked.

"Yeah, they found it mostly buried, but not very well, and not very far away, like someone wanted it to be found."

Craig raised his eyebrows again and looked at Emma and then back to Hawk.

Hawk held up a hand and said "Before I go any further Craig, tell me your thoughts here. Do you have any suspicions into who shot you?"

Craig looked at Emma again, but it lacked heat this time.

"Yes," he said staring flatly at Emma. "Norman Foster did, I'm sure."

Emma winced. God knew she shouldn't feel responsible for Norman's actions but she did.

"There's something I need to tell you Emma, or did you tell her already Hawk?"

"About Norman visiting you? No, I didn't."

Emma looked from Hawk to Craig, trepidation building in her brain. She didn't want to hear this. But of course she was going to.

"Norman came to visit me at the fire station. He threatened me and told me to stay away from you. He almost pulled out his gun. Then he told me you were a cocaine-addicted whore."

Emma froze. She felt herself flush hot. A whore? What in the hell?

Craig continued, "I told him I knew he was full of shit and I tried to fight him. Frankie broke us up."

Emma bit her lip, trying not to cry. She didn't know how to feel. Her ex-husband was never going to leave her alone. He was telling people the worst things she had ever heard in her life. Craig had been mad at her when that happened, but he had still stuck up for her. And he may have gotten himself shot because of it.

Craig looked back at Hawk. "Any chance Norman knows I'm FBI?"

Hawk nodded. "A good chance actually. That's why I didn't want you in on this case to begin with. And that's why I put you in the fire department instead of the police department when you insisted."

Craig nodded and addressed Emma. "Look, I know what you are thinking. You are thinking that it's your fault that I got shot, if indeed it was Norman who shot me. I want to tell you two things. One, it's not your fault. Two, nothing Norman does is your fault."

Emma nodded, still sure it was her fault in

her head. It was like lightening, searing her from the inside. She dropped her face to her hands and wiped back the tears that were spilling silently over.

Hawk came over and put a hand on Emma's shoulder. "He's right you know. It's not your fault. Norman's unpredictable and trigger happy."

Emma nodded into her hands, still not convinced.

Hawk continued. "Ok, so you slept on, and then Emma showed up. The agents at the door tried to turn her away but she wouldn't have it. They called me and we had a little talk. I learned what had happened to her and decided she was probably as high on the hit list as you are, so I got her a cot in your room. She's been here ever since."

Craig looked at Emma again. She got another slight smile. She gave him one back, still feeling numb and horrible.

"Yesterday morning, I got a little piece of news from the lab. Guess whose fingerprints are on the gun." He turned to Craig expectantly.

Craig bit. "Mine?"

Emma and Hawk both laughed at this and Hawk shook his head.

"No, Ok," he leaned back a bit in the bed, thinking. After a few minutes, Emma realized his breathing was deep and relaxed.

"Craig?" she said softly.

She crossed the room and touched his hand. He was asleep. She turned off the light above the bed and motioned to Hawk. They went out in the hall.

"I want you to stay here again tonight Emma."

Emma nodded. "OK."

"The doctor said he'll be moved to a new room in the morning if everything goes well. He doesn't need to be in the ICU anymore."

"Will he still have guards?" Emma asked, looking at Adrian and Bret, sitting close by.

"Yes, until we know for sure who did this and that person is arrested, you and he both need guards."

Emma hugged her arms to her body, feeling suddenly chilled. "OK, want me to call you if he wakes again?"

"Yes please." Hawk gave her a stiff, one-handed hug, checked in with his agents, and walked down the hall to the exit.

Emma pushed back in to the room. She sat upright next to Craig's bed all night, occasionally cat-napping, with his big hand held in her smaller one. He didn't wake again that night.

Chapter 10

Norman's skin was crawling. He hated feeling like this. Out of control. He had started to put his plan to get rid of Masterson into effect, but when he called his second contact at the hospital, he found out Masterson wasn't awake yet and his contact had no reason or no way to get in or out of his room until Masterson woke. But once Masterson woke, things could be all over for Norman.

The doctor had no reason to get into his room either, and the doctor wouldn't do what he wanted anyway. Norman prided himself on his judge of character, and he judged the doctor would rather go down for the cocaine charge than be an accomplice to murder.

Norman had been careful, and there should be nothing Masterson could recall that would pin the crime on him, but you never knew. Those FBI guys were slick. He'd also done his level best to frame Emma for the crime, but he hadn't seen Emma at her house in days. From what he could tell she was with Masterson. No one had arrested her yet. And they would have already found the gun, wouldn't they have?

Norman paced through his sparsely-furnished living room, looking out the window every time he passed it. He knew what he was expecting, but he was trying desperately to deny it to himself. He was expecting the FBI to come to his house and arrest him.

How had things gotten so out of control, so quickly? He pondered whether the Senator could get him out of this mess. *Would* the senator get him out of this mess? If the Senator was president he could pardon anyone he wanted - but the senator wasn't making a presidential bid for 2 more years.

Think man, think! There has to be a way out!

He could make it very clear to the senator that if he went down, the senator was going down with him. But that would mean confessing to a lot of crimes they probably couldn't pin on him right now. But the senator didn't know that.

Norman punched himself in the side of the head, hard. He saw stars. *He needed to get a look at the files and know what the FBI knew!* But his hacker friend had found no files to access. Nothing related to any investigation in Westwood Harbor or having anything to do with Emma Hill or Craig Masterson or Craig MacDonnell. On a whim, Norman had him check files by Holden Kinkaid and found nothing over the last 2 years. But Kinkaid was still an agent. Norman wondered if they were so deep undercover none of their files were being entered into the network. It was possible if they suspected computer hacking.

Norman started to think he needed to prepare for the inevitable. If the FBI closed in on him, maybe the best thing to do would be to just run. To take off and build a new life somewhere else. He could even leave the country if he needed to. That might be his best bet if the FBI were looking for him. He toyed with this idea. Brazil, Paraguay, Spain Sweden, Japan? He would be leaving everything he worked for behind, but it would be better than being in jail. And what about Emma?

If he were going to have to pull this off he would need some time to get away. How could he buy himself some time? Norman's mind started churning. If the bomb were dropped, and the FBI closed in on him, what could give him time to get away? He didn't want to leave now. There was still a chance this could all work out in his favor.

He looked around his house, thinking about what would happen if the FBI decided to arrest him. They would most likely do it here, where he was relaxed. Almost certainly they wouldn't do it at work where he would be guaranteed to have his guns on him. How could he make that work in his favor? If the FBI showed up at his doorstop. The beginnings of a plan formed in his mind.

Norman's phone rang, interrupting his musings. He picked it up.

"Captain Foster, you wanted me to call you if anything changed with Craig Masterson." It was Dr. Paloma.

"Yes, what has changed?" Dread and excitement crept into Norman's bones in equal measure.

"2 things. His status has been changed from guarded to stable, and he is being moved from the ICU to a recovery room. I can't find out where though until they actually move him. It should happen in the morning. And he still has his guards."

Norman's mind raced. He was getting better. He was going to live. In the new room Norman's other contact at the hospital could probably get to him.

"Perfect. Is that it?" Norman barked.

"Well, there is one more thing. I don't know anything about it because I still haven't been able to get a look at his chart, but the nurse I talked to said he has amnesia. She didn't know how extensive it was."

"Amnesia!" Norman felt a giggle building up inside him.

"Yes, some sort of amnesia."

Norman laughed. "Thank you Doctor. You've done a good job. You can consider that debt of your's almost paid off." He hung up the phone.

Norman stopped pacing. He went into the kitchen, whistling. All his doubts fell away. For the first time in several days he felt like the whole world was on his side. Like God himself was smiling down upon him. A thought struck him. Maybe God was ensuring he had another chance to get this right. *Well don't worry, Big Guy, this time it's going to stick.*

Chapter 11

Dimly, Emma was aware of nurses entering during the night. She slept on and off, sometimes getting up to rearrange Craig's pillows or massage his legs.

As the early light filtered through the window, she took her spot again next to his bed, and grasped his hand, laying her head back for a bit more rest.

She woke again, feeling like she was missing something. Her hand was empty. She sat up quickly, opening her eyes. Craig was watching her, his hands folded in his lap. "Your fingerprints are on the gun, aren't they?" he asked without smiling.

She tried to smile, but foreboding filled her. "You FBI guys are pretty smart," she joked, feebly.

He looked at the clock on the wall, and then towards the door.

Emma wanted to jump out of the chair and cover him with kisses. She wanted to cry and tell him how scared she had been. She wished he would look at her and say something, anything.

"So, Emma," he began, but trailed off.

All of a sudden she was scared to death of what was going to come out of his mouth. Was she going to lose him again, a 4th time?

He looked at his hands and said, "I wanted to say thanks for coming to find me."

Her eyes teared. Well that wasn't so bad. She opened her mouth to speak but he went on.

"I don't remember what happened that night. Hawk says I forgave you. I wanted to forgive you before anything happened but I wasn't able to find that place in my heart again, where things felt good between us." He rushed on, seeming to want to get everything out before she said anything. "I've been awake for a while now, watching you sleep. You really are a lovely, wonderful person, but I still haven't found that place. I really can't thank you enough for saving my life, and I do believe you that I forgave you, but until I remember it for myself ..."

He looked at her, openly, waiting.

She nodded and bit her lip, her throat clogged with her own heartache. "I know Craig," she whispered.

"But I'm definitely not mad anymore. I was mad you know, after you asked Dennis out. But that has fallen away. I just don't feel, you know."

"I do know Craig." She felt like her heart would burst. But there was still a chance. Actually there were two chances. She could win him back, or he could remember. She turned her emotions away from the despair filling her body and tried to focus on the road ahead.

"Friends?" he asked with a small smile.

"Friends," she declared, with more enthusiasm than she felt.

The door opened and a petite nurse in fresh, green scrubs entered. "Mr. Masterson, you are being moved to your new room."

"Now?" he asked.

"Right now, she smiled. "We will move you down there in this bed. Once we get there, you try to walk. If you can walk, I can get rid of some of these wires running out of you. If we can get rid of some of these wires, you get lunch today."

"Real food!" Craig rubbed his hands together in anticipation. "I'll run for a big steak and a Coke."

Emma couldn't believe this was happening so fast! They were asking him to walk? He really must be getting better quickly. She ran and started gathering her stuff.

The nurse piled all of Craig's stuff on his bed, unlocked the bed, and rolled it towards the door. She motioned to Emma, "Can you push that?" indicating his heart monitor.

Emma grabbed it and followed.

They went to the elevator and the two FBI guards followed. Emma whipped out Craig's phone and texted Hawk. *Moving, not sure where yet.*

The nurse led them all to the new room and helped them get set up. It had an extra bed in it, but the nurse assured them he wouldn't have a roommate. Emma wondered if she would be allowed to sleep there. Emma texted Hawk the new room number.

The nurse asked Emma to leave the room while she tried to get Craig moving. Another nurse came in with a walker as Emma was slipping out the door.

Emma ran quickly down to the vending

machine and grabbed herself some food. By the time she came back, the second nurse was leaving and said she could go back in.

She pushed the door open and saw Craig sitting in the bed, big chest exposed as his hospital gown fell open to the waist The sight of his chest stirred her emotions. She wanted to touch him and kiss him so badly. The bandage on his face reminded her that even if he was willing, he was still injured.

"Did you do it?"

He beamed at her, both dimples in full force. "I walked! And look, I have a bathroom!"

"Yay!" she clapped her hands like a little girl. He was going to be OK. "Are you in any pain?"

"Yeah, my head hurts, but it's bearable. And my tongue feels all weird in my mouth. I keep accidentally chewing on it."

The phone in Emma's pocket buzzed. Hawk was on his way up. She slipped it back in her pocket and it buzzed again. Jerry and Vivian were on their way over.

"Craig, can Jerry come by with his new girlfriend? Would that bother you? Because if it would I could just meet them in the cafeteria."

"No that wouldn't bother me at all." He carefully arranged his sheets so his legs and stomach were fully covered.

Emma texted Jerry, come to room 417. Craig walked!

Emma looked up at the door opening - Hawk. "Craig walked!" she cried. Hawk beamed and went to the bedside to shake Craig's hand

and give him a hug. Emma knew Hawk was probably even more excited than she was, but he was good at keeping those emotions in.

Emma slid into a chair, hugging herself. She was content, for now. Craig was on the mend, and she couldn't ask for much more than that. *Just that he would love me again.* She pushed that thought away.

A knock on the door pulled her out of her reverie. She opened it and Jerry slid in the room. He looked over at Craig and smiled then whispered to Emma, "Vivian is waiting outside. She felt embarrassed to come in since she doesn't even know Craig."

"Oh that's silly!" Emma pulled the door partially open. "I am going to bring her in."

"Ok," Jerry said, "Good luck, and just so you know, we're not really a romantic item anymore. We had the talk last night and decided we are just going to be friends, but I told her she could hang out with me still. Her birthday is coming up and she didn't want to celebrate it alone in a strange town."

At the mention of a birthday Emma had a strange niggling in the back of her head. Her birthday was this month too. She hadn't even thought of it with everything that was going on. What day was it? She pushed the thoughts away as not important.

"Already Jerry? That's too bad. I really liked her."

"I know, she's a sweet girl, but you can't force it if it doesn't fit."

"True, true," Emma said, slipping out the

door. She heard Jerry's hearty "Craig! You look great!" from behind her.

She looked around and spotted Vivian leaning against the wall halfway down the hall. She ran down. "Vivian! Hi!"

Vivian smiled shyly. "Hi Emma, sorry I didn't come in. I didn't want to intrude."

Emma was struck again by her eyes. The light blue, so much like her own light blue, contrasted with Vivian's skin, making her look extremely beautiful and unique. *Is that what people think when they look at me?*

"No intrusion. I'm so happy you're here. You should come meet my, well, uh, he's not really my boyfriend but I hope he will be soon." Emma pulled Vivian by the hand towards the door, past the two guards.

"Emma, you should know, Jerry and I are just friends. We aren't dating anymore."

"I know silly, he told me, but that doesn't matter." Emma pulled her into the room.

Hawk and Jerry were laughing by the head of the bed, obviously at Craig's expense. He was putting on a show of being upset with them but Emma could tell he wasn't. Emma was glad that Hawk and Jerry were getting along already. She was already thinking of Hawk as one of her friends. She wasn't surprised though. Jerry got along with most everyone, especially cops and firefighters.

She pulled Vivian close to the bed and introduced her to Craig and Hawk as 'my friend, Vivian.' Everyone said hello and nice to meet you and Emma noticed Vivian's wide-set, lovely eyes looked even more nervous now, darting around the room and looking down constantly, lighting occasionally on Hawk. She tried to make her new friend feel at ease.

"Vivian, when's your birthday?"

"It's tomorrow."

Emma thought for a second, her brow furrowing. "What's the date tomorrow?"

"It's the 13th."

The men were talking and joking again at the head of the bed. Their voices fell away. Emma's reality shrunk down to just her and Vivian. Tingles marched up and down her neck and scalp, her hair trying to stand on edge.

"How old are you going to be?" Emma asked, her voice sounding tiny and strained in her own ears.

"31, why, Emma, what's wrong?" Vivian grabbed her hand, concerned.

Emma didn't know what she looked like. Probably white as a sheet. She felt like she was about to pass out, or maybe puke.

"Vivian, where were you born?"

"Right here in Westwood General Hospital, actually."

Emma knew. Her heart knew and it was telling her body. Only her brain needed to confirm it. "D-Did you have a twin sister that you were separated from at birth?" Emma had to force out the last words. She was choking on them.

"Oh my God. Oh my God." Realization dawned on Vivian's face. She grabbed Emma's other hand. Her mouth dropped open. A wail of excitement built up in her throat, sounding almost like a train whistle. "Oh my God!"

She threw her arms around Emma's neck and started sobbing. The tears flowed just as freely down Emma's cheeks. Emma laughed and sobbed at the same time. She hugged her sister back and cried out 30 years of separation.

The men looked at them, mouths open. They hadn't been following the conversation. Not one of them could imagine what the two women were crying and laughing and shrieking about.

Emma pulled back, grasping her sister's face. "That's why we have the same eyes!" At the same time, Vivian put her hands up to Emma's eyes and said, "I thought you were so lovely and interesting when we met and I so wanted to get to know you better. No wonder!"

Emma hugged her again. "I was fascinated with you too. We knew, we recognized each other!"

Jerry interrupted. "Do you two want to tell us what's going on here?"

Emma turned to them, her arm slung around Vivian's shoulders as though she never wanted to stop touching her. "Guys, you are looking at two twin sisters separated at birth, if you can believe it!"

"But, you guys don't really look alike, except the eyes," Hawk said, frowning.

"Yep, we're fraternal twins," Vivian said.

Emma turned back to Vivian, wanting to hash out what Vivian knew and didn't know about their parents and their birth, Craig forgotten for the moment. "We should go somewhere. Want to have lunch at the cafeteria?"

"Yes, OK," Vivian smiled teasingly, "Sis."

Emma threw her head back and laughed. "I have a sister!" she cried, exuberant. The two women walked out, arms around each other, leaving the three men still trying to understand what had happened.

Chapter 12

Hawk turned to Craig. "Did you know she had a twin sister?" Craig shook his head no, mouth still open.

"You?" Hawk asked, turning to Jerry. "Well, yeah, I knew Emma had a twin sister, but I didn't know that Vivian did. No wonder I was so attracted to her at the library. She must have reminded me of Emma."

Craig's eyes narrowed. "You have a thing for Emma?"

Jerry put his hand up, laughing. "No man, I love her like a little sister though. I think she's one of the most amazing women on the planet."

Craig nodded, satisfied.

The door opened and a nurse came in. "Mr. Masterson, since you are doing so well the doctor said you can try eating some solid food," she sang out in a lilting voice.

Craig stopped and wondered if he was hungry. Yes, he was a little, but he was more tired than anything. This morning had really zapped his strength.

He did want to try some solid food though. He couldn't wait to get all his strength back and get out of this bed. He was incredibly appreciative for the amazing medical care he had received but couldn't wait till he walked out of the hospital and back into his active life.

Hawk and Jerry sat down, the three men

joking with each other like long-time friends.

The nurse did her checks, admonished Hawk and Jerry they'd have to leave for some quiet time after Craig ate, told them the food would be coming up shortly, and left the room. Craig rubbed the side of his face over the bandage. His skin itched horribly. Now that he had thought of food, he felt ravenous, almost weak with hunger.

A knock on the door signaled the arrival of a man pushing a rolling tray into the room, an appetizing smell preceding him. Hawk watched him carefully. He was a small man, no more than about 5 and a half feet tall. He was slim with a pinched face. His gaze jumped from the three men in the room to the walls, the food, anything but the patient in the bed.

"That smells great," Craig said.

The man wiped his mouth and opened it, then closing it. He pushed the tray to the bed and took off all the lids and plastic wrap. He raised his hand to his forehead in a little salute and said "Well, there you go," and rushed out of the room.

"That was weird," Hawk remarked, forehead furrowed.

"Yeah, he's a strange one," Jerry remarked. "He's never been the same since his time in prison."

Hawk's eyes narrowed fiercely. "You know him?"

"Know of him. Miller's the name. I treated him a few times when he was an addict. He went to prison for a bit and I haven't had to treat him since, but I see him sometimes here in the hospital."

Craig's stomach rumbled loudly. Hawk turned to watch him. His dinner was chicken smothered in some kind of white gravy, plus green beans in a butter sauce. Craig cut a piece of chicken first with a knife and a fork and tunneled it towards his mouth. Some of the gravy fell off the chicken onto his bare chest. "Ow, hot!" He put the fork down and wiped the gravy off his chest, then picked the fork back up, heading the chicken back towards his mouth.

A look of terror on his face, Hawk took a big step forward and slapped the fork and the chicken out of Craig's hand. The fork flew across the room and clattered into the corner.

"What?" Craig asked, immediately alert.

Jerry sat up straighter and gaped at them.

"Look at your chest where the gravy was."

Craig looked down. "That dirty son of a bitch," he snarled.

"What? What?" Jerry looked too but didn't know what he was looking at. "Did the gravy leave that brown spot on his skin?"

"That brown mark was probably caused by a new, industrial type of poison called mollhem. It marks the skin on the outside, but is otherwise almost undetectable, especially if you don't know what you are looking for. Drug dealers in Europe developed it but it hasn't gained much of a foothold here in the U.S. yet. It has to go in a watery food, like a drink, gravy, sauce, or soup. It's totally tasteless and doesn't make the mouth burn for an hour or two." Hawk's voice was tight and mean.

"What would have happened if he would have eaten that?" Jerry asked.

"If it's in all of this food and the drink, this is enough to kill him by stopping his heart in about 45 minutes."

Jerry whistled appreciatively. "Good thing you were here."

"Good thing you were here Jerry, and good thing Craig spilled his food. I wouldn't have been suspicious if you hadn't said Miller had been to prison, and I still might not have stopped him from eating it if I hadn't seen the mark on his skin."

Hawk pulled out his phone and sent a text.

"Um, Jerry, we've got some business to discuss here. Do you think you could ...?"

"Sure, sure, I'll go check on the girls." Jerry shook Craig's hand again. "It sure is good to see you doing good. I thought Emma was going to die of worry."

"Thanks man," Craig said.

As Jerry was leaving another man came in and handed Hawk some bags. He started bagging up all of Craig's food. "From now on, you don't eat anything unless it comes straight from me."

"Got it boss. So are we guessing who was behind this? And what are you going to do about that Miller guy?"

"My guess is on Foster. How about you? Remembered anything yet?"

Craig shook his head. "Nothing. But I'm betting on Foster too."

Hawk nodded. "I'll get this stuff tested and then arrest that Miller guy myself. Hopefully I get some answers from him. I think we are going to have to move on Foster in the next few days. We can't wait for more evidence linking him and the Senator. Norman Foster is getting too dangerous."

Still hungry, but also tired, Craig felt himself dozing off a little. He fought it and went with it equally. There was so much more to talk about, but he needed to rest. He could feel sleep pulling him, lulling him, taking over ...

***

When Craig awoke it was dark and quiet. His room seemed empty. *Where was everyone? Where were all his friends now?* His mind replayed a dream he had been having. He relaxed into it, and walked that line between awake and asleep gently, without reaching too hard.

He was walking in the dirt, picking his big boots up over the tangle of blackened, charred branches. Something was poking him mercilessly in the lower back. Poke. Jab. He felt confused. Someone was behind him, poking him hard with something and urging him onwards. He had a sense of a large man behind him. A man as tall as he was.

The man directed him into a forest with the object in his back, like he was turning a rudder on a boat. Something else was wrong. Had the man spoken? Everything felt surreal, strange. The man spoke. Craig didn't recognize the voice. It was high and reedy. "Where are all your friends now FBI man?" Craig knew this was bad news. The worst news. He calculated his chances of getting away if he ran. Slim to none probably. He was about to take his chances and turn around to fight when the voice said "I wonder how your pretty little paramedic is doing?" Craig froze in mid-step. "Seems to me she she shouldn't have to spend any more time out in these woods tonight. Didn't you already save her once?" Craig's eyes scanned the forest. Was Emma out here? "It would be a shame if she was helpless in one of those buildings and the fire swept through here." Jab jab. Craig was urged on again with what he was sure was a very large gun in his back.

Craig was pushed towards the entrance of a hunter's shack. His eyes searched the inside in the meager light. He didn't see anything. Was Emma really out here? "What do you want from me?" he asked the man behind him.

"Oh nothing, just your soul." The voice laughed and the night exploded. Craig was knocked over onto the dirt floor of the open shack by the force of a bullet slamming into his back. He knew the vest had caught it, but it still felt like it shattered some ribs. He clawed the ground, trying to get up and get around behind him but immediately the night exploded again. This time he was down. He couldn't move. Couldn't even think. Dimly he was aware of heat and smoke and pressure on top of him. He felt cold, then searing hot, then colder than he'd ever been in his life. His muscles would not obey his commands. It became hard to think. He floated.

He thought of Emma. Sweet, sweet Emma. She was safe, she had to be. He couldn't save her if she wasn't.

Craig drifted off to sleep again, thinking in his mind that he needed to talk to Hawk, and to Emma.

Chapter 13

"It's midnight Emma, we've been here for hours."

Emma and Vivian were lounging on the couches in the lobby, having long ago abandoned the cafeteria as uncomfortable.

"I know Viv, do you feel tired?"

Vivan shook her head no, and then sucked in her breath. Emma followed her line of sight. Hawk was approaching them from the other end of the wide corridor. His heavy work boots slammed into the thin carpet with every step he took. Emma looked at her sister curiously. She was openly staring and biting on her thumbnail. Was she taken with Hawk? Emma looked back at Hawk. Sure he was handsome, in a dark and dangerous sort of way. His dark hair was cropped close to his skull in a neat, military haircut. His eyes flashed and took in everything around him. He was scowling slightly, like he was about to scold them, the scowl accentuating his strong jaw. His T-shirt and jeans clung to him tightly, showing off his strong chest and legs like tree trunks. Where Craig was fair, Hawk was dark, but equally handsome.

When he reached the couch he said "Emma, you are going to stay in the hospital, right?"

"Yep." She gave him a smile and looked at her sister. She was looking at the ground.

"Good. When are you heading back up to Craig's room?"

Craig! Emma jumped to her feet. "Is he OK?"

"Yes, he's sleeping, he has been for hours."

"Oh thank goodness. I'm not sure when we'll be done here. We have a lot to catch up on, don't we Viv?"

Her sister mumbled something but still looked at the floor. Hawk gave Vivian a hard glance and nodded at Emma. "I'm heading down to get some shut-eye. Message me if you need me."

Emma nodded. When he was gone, she sat back down and asked her sister "What was that about?"

Vivian giggled uncharacteristically, or so Emma thought. She didn't know her sister well enough yet to know what was characteristic or not.

"I don't know. He makes me feel like I'm 12 and late for gym class or something." Vivian breathed.

"Yeah, he's a commanding figure for sure. Are you sure you don't, you know, like him or something?"

"No, don't be silly. I don't even know him. He is handsome though."

Emma fell silent for a moment. "So whatever happened with you and Jerry?"

"Oh I don't know. He's not totally my type, but I said I would go out with him because he seemed so sweet and genuine. And I was lonely here. But the same thing always happens. I like cops and firefighters - really manly men, you know? But they don't like me for very long. I think I intimidate them or something. I don't mean to and I don't try to. I just do. I'm not sure if it's because I have a lot of money so they think I'm spoiled, or if my job title makes them think I'm super smart and looking down on them. Which I'm not." She frowned and played with a thread on the couch, sounding miserable.

"But I'm glad I met Jerry, he's such a sweetie, and he's your partner. It's such a huge, wonderful coincidence." She smiled at Emma and tugged at her hand laughing. "I still can't believe we found each other."

Emma smiled. "I know, me neither. So why are you in town? Why were you at the library?"

"Oh, Vivian's face darkened. I actually am here looking up our family tree, or trying to. I have a disease."

"No!" Emma tightened her hold on Vivian's hand. "What kind of a disease?"

It's called a desmoid tumor, and it's in my abdomen. It's a kind of cancer. It's pretty harmless right now, but my doctor and I are trying to develop a treatment plan for it. I need to know my family history to know the best way to treat it. Since I am adopted, I don't know anything about either side of my family. I came here to Westwood Harbor to try to uncover them."

She smiled. "And now I have a sister."

Fear gripped Emma. Cancer? Was she

going to lose someone else so quickly?

Vivian peered in her face, noting her concern. "Don't worry sweetie, it's not spreading and it's not doing anything to me right now. My doctor gave me a 95% chance of beating it completely within the next 5 years, but we aren't even going to start treating it until it spreads a little." She leaned in close. "I'm OK sis."

Emma nodded, close to tears. She wiped her eyes. "So have you discovered anything? I don't even know our mom's name. It was just Jane Doe on the birth certificate when I went to the records office to check. I don't know how truthful the state records guy was with me when I went to see the original though, he just read it off to me. He wouldn't let me see it."

"I saw mine. It says Jane Doe." Vivian said.

Emma nodded sadly. "How do you even start looking for family members when you don't even know your mom's name?"

"I bet your FBI friend could help us." Vivian whispered, looking longingly down the corridor where Hawk had disappeared.

Emma hadn't even thought of this. "I bet he could! When this is all over we'll have to ask him."

Vivian beamed. "Yes!"

***

Craig opened his eyes wide and looked around, disoriented. The clock said 8 a.m. Light was streaming in the windows. He felt good.

Strong. And something else was different. He looked to his right. Emma was sleeping above the covers on the bed next to him, fully clothed. Emma. He remembered. He remembered everything. He had forgiven her fully. The emotions flooded him. He wanted to take her in his arms and seal everything with a kiss, and then more kisses, down her neck, down her body. Uh Oh. Craig rearranged his sheets so if a nurse came in she couldn't see the physical sign of his thoughts about Emma.

He got up and used the bathroom, pulling his heart monitor and IV bag along with him on the pole. His head didn't hurt anymore, at least not much. He wondered if he was strong enough for *that* kind of physical exertion. Emma's sleeping form called to him, her hips rounded and feminine on the bed as she lay on her side.

When he came out of the bathroom she was there, standing outside of the door.

"Craig, are you OK, do you need help?" Her hair deliciously mussed, large blue eyes peering at him worriedly. She looked more lovely than he had ever seen her. He reached out with the arm that didn't have an IV in it and tucked an unruly piece of hair behind her ear.

Her eyes widened and a soft "oh" escaped her lips. He hadn't touched her purposely since he had come out of the coma. He needed to make up for that. He smiled and ran his hand through her hair, softly taking a large handful and pulling her to him. She melted in his embrace. He lowered his head to hers. "Emma, how could I have forgotten that I am falling in love with you?

You are so very lovable," he whispered into her parted lips. She sighed and searched his lips out with hers, closing his eyes. He saw a tear roll down her right cheek before he lost himself in the moment.

When he finally, reluctantly, pulled back she opened her eyes. "You remember."

"I do." He smiled at her again, drinking in everything about her face.

"Do you remember who shot you?"

"Well, he was very careful, so no, I don't."

"Did he say anything?" She was distracting him, running her fingers through his hair and pressing her body against his.

"Yes, but I think he had some sort of a voice changer. His voice sounded strange. It didn't sound like Norman if that's what you're wondering. I'll tell you the full story when Hawk gets up here. Maybe he can come up with something."

The door opened with a whoosh. A nurse came in and eyed them accusingly. "You seem to be feeling better Mr. Masterson?"

"Way better," he said with a chuckle. Emma giggled into his neck.

"Well I need to check your bandages, so if you could?" The nurse motioned to the bed.

Craig reluctantly pulled away from Emma and headed over, being very careful to hold his gown together and away from his body. The nurse was already irritated enough, she didn't need a look at the evidence of his arousal. She'd probably faint.

"I'll text Hawk," Emma said. Craig

nodded.

The nurse finished her business and left the room. Hawk came in with a haggard smile for both of them.

"Hawk, Craig remembers everything."

Hawk turned to Craig, excitement in his eyes. "Was it Foster?"

Craig shook his head. "Not sure buddy, sorry. It probably was but he was very careful. He used a voice changer and everything."

"Damn!"

Hawk settled in and Craig told them both exactly what had happened that night, starting with putting Emma in the helicopter and then heading over to wildfire scene. He had been working with a partner, but they had been on different sides of the active firebreak. A bulldozer had come through, then the firefighters on the ground were setting burn backs on each side. Craig had been working his area single-mindedly. It was loud and hot and visibility was low. Someone came up behind him and shoved a gun in his back and prodded him towards the forest.

He finished the story and they all picked it apart for unanswered questions. None of them found anything out that would definitively pin it on Norman.

"There's one thing that's been bothering me for a while," Emma said. "I don't own a gun. So how did a gun with my fingerprints on it get at the scene?"

"Have you ever shot a gun?" Hawk asked, turning to her with an interested look on her face.

"Yes, of course, in the Army, but not a handgun. What kind of a gun was it?"

"It was a 9mm Smith and Wesson 5906."

Emma thought for a second. "I went shooting with Norman a few times," she said softly, trying to remember.

"Was this when you were married?" Hawk asked, excitedly.

"Yep, 7 years ago," Emma said, grimacing. She didn't want to think of the implications of this. If Norman had given her a gun in such a way that only her fingerprints were on it, and then kept it pristine like that for 7 years, well that would mean so many crazy things about him. Things she could barely comprehend.

Hawk sat in silence, deep in thought. Emma didn't want to interrupt him.

He leaned forward suddenly and plied her for details of every time they went shooting. Emma tried to remember but it was hard; that was a long time ago.

Eventually satisfied, Hawk excused himself and said he'd be back. He had some work to do.

"Emma, I'm starving."

"Oh yeah? Starving for?" she trailed off, a mischievous smile playing around her lips. She walked over to his bed and ran her fingers down his bare chest in between the two halves of the gown.

He growled and grabbed her around the waist, pulling her onto the bed. "Starving for a big plate of bacon and eggs that I can eat off of your bare ass."

"Ewwww, gross." Emma laughed.

The door whooshed open again and Emma quickly climbed off the bed. There was no privacy in a hospital.

Craig's doctor strolled in. A small man with small hands and thinning red hair. "Good morning Mr. Masterson, I hear you are feeling better," he remarked with a twinkle in his eye.

Emma blushed and moved away from the bed. She went in the corner to text Vivian.

"Loads better Doc, now when can I get out of here?"

"Patience sir, patience. Let's see how you are looking."

The doctor did an examination first, and then asked Craig to lie down while he peeked under both bandages. He stepped back and said, "I have some good news."

"Oh yeah, let's hear it."

"You are healing up perfectly. If you have someone to take care of you and you promise to come back for advanced recovery, you can leave tomorrow."

Emma's eyes lit up in the corner. Tomorrow? *I wonder if he'll be able to exert himself?* She blushed a little, but not enough to stop the thought. She imagined taking him home to her place and taking care of him, naked. Or maybe in one of those little french maid outfits. She didn't have a french maid outfit, but maybe she could pick one up.

Craig must have been thinking the same thing. "Are there any, um, limitations on my activities doc?"

The doctor raised an eyebrow. "If you mean weightlifting yes, don't do it. If you mean work, you can't go back to work for at least 10 days. If you mean anything else, no, there are no limitations. If it hurts, don't do it. If it doesn't hurt, it's fine. You are in excellent physical condition, and as such your body is healing quite quickly."

"Thanks doc."

The doctor left and Emma ran back over to the bed.

"You heard what the doctor said, you need someone to take care of you. I volunteer."

"OK, but I plan on spending a lot of my recovery time in bed." He pulled her onto the hospital bed again and kissed her hard, deeply, giving her a taste of what was to come.

She nibbled on his bottom lip and ran her hands across his broad, sculpted chest, leaning over to straddle him but careful not to tangle in his IV wires. His heart monitor had long since been removed. "The doctor said you were in fine physical condition. I'll have to check that out for myself."

The phone in her pocked buzzed. "Argh." She looked. "It's Vivian, she's on her way up. This will have to wait some more." She swung her leg off of him and climbed down.

"So is she really your twin sister Emma?"

"Yes, she is. Our mother died in childbirth and the hospital didn't know her name so we were made wards of the state. Vivian was adopted but I entered the foster system."

"Wow, I can't believe the family who adopted your sister didn't take you both."

Emma hadn't even considered that. Who does that? For an instant her vision darkened with thoughts of what could have been. But then she shook her head. *No reason to go down that path*, she chided herself. *I'm sure they had a good reason. Maybe they couldn't afford more than one baby.* But wait, Vivian had said her parents were loaded. She actually had a trust fund and didn't have to work a day in her life if she didn't want to. But she did want to, because she was innately driven and curious and she loved her job. *Maybe they just didn't know. Maybe the state had only offered them one baby.* That seemed more likely.

Emma shook her head and focused on Craig.

"Yeah, that's weird, but maybe they didn't know about me."

A knock on the door caused them both to look up. Vivian pushed it slightly open and peeked in.

"Hi Viv, come in! Come in!" Emma was so excited to see her. She finally had a family member. She turned to Craig. "Think they'll let you go down to the cafeteria? Or should we bring you up some food?"

"Bring me up some food? A huge plate of meat and eggs would be great with some juice. I need to wait here for Hawk. He said he had something he needed to discuss with me."

At the mention of Hawk, Vivian blushed and looked to the door as if she were hoping to see him. Emma's eyes grew wide and she laughed to herself, *boy she's got it bad.* "Vivian can we go get some food? I haven't eaten yet either."

Vivian nodded, smiling, relaxed again.

The door opened again and Hawk strode in confidently, heavy boots eating up the tiled floor, clipboard under one arm. He flipped on all the light switches, smiled at Emma, completely ignored Vivian, and gruffly said "Good you're up," to Craig.

Craig raised an eyebrow. Hawk moved on to the window and threw the curtains wide, letting in the light. He took one of the room's two chairs and pulled it close to Craig's bed and sat down, pulling a pen from the clipboard and beginning to scribble furiously.

Emma looked at Vivian. Vivian wore an irritated look and was looking at Hawk with fire in her eyes. "Good morning, *Hawk,*" she said.

Hawk's pen stopped scribbling and he looked up briefly. "Morn," he grunted and went back to his clipboard and papers.

"Wow, some people" Vivian breathed under her breath, and turned on her heel, heading for the door.

Emma shot Craig a questioning glance. He raised his hands to his shoulders in an I-don't-know gesture. Then he motioned for her to come over to him. When she got there he hugged her and kissed her on the cheek and whispered "I'll ask," in her ear.

She pressed her lips to his, then ran after her sister.

***

"What was that about man?"

Hawk raised his head and looked at Craig, feigning ignorance. "What?"

"Why were you so rude to Emma's sister?"

"Was I rude to her?"

"It looked like you were from here."

"Hmph, sorry." Hawk turned back to his papers.

Craig studied him for a moment. What was going on here? It wasn't like Hawk to be mean to anyone.

"No really, do you know her or something about her?"

"Look, we really have to talk about business," Hawk snarled, leaving no room for argument.

"Ok, great, so just clear this up and then we can." Craig had been friends with him for too long to be scared off with one of his distancing tactics.

Hawk sighed heavily. "No, I don't know her, but I know her *type*. Everything about her screams rich, spoiled brat. From her designer shoes to her expensive hair cut and diamond earrings. I spent most of my childhood with girls like that, and dated a few when I was older. There ain't nothing good about them. I don't like to hang out with trust-fund babies."

"Lucy was a trust-fund baby."

"Yeah, but Lucy was different. You of all people should know that!" Hawk stood up and threw his clipboard on his chair. "I'm getting a drink." He stormed out.

"OK then," Craig said into the empty room. Sore subject apparently. Craig's family didn't have near the money that Hawk's family had and the two had not been in the same social circles or even went to the same schools. Craig worked summers as a lifeguard at the country club Hawk's family frequented. They met when they were both 16. Hawk had seemed to go out of his way to befriend Craig, and Craig was thrilled to be his friend. Most of the boys in the club treated Craig with disdain. They had become fast friends, doing everything together, including joining the Army at 18 for a four year stint. Craig and Hawk had taken all their leave together, spending these vacations at Hawk's place. Craig had always had a crush on Hawk's little sister, Lucy, but it wasn't until she turned 18 and Craig and Hawk were 20 that Craig finally asked her out. Hawk never had let his parents give him anything, always wanting to work for it himself. Always seeming to have something to prove.

Craig wondered if there was something about his friend that he didn't know very well. He tried to think back to girls Hawk had dated from back home. He could only think of a few, and none that were serious. He'd had a girlfriend in the Army that got pretty serious, but when she switched duty stations they had broken up. Since then, Craig couldn't think of one serious girlfriend.

Hawk interrupted his thoughts by coming back in the room with a Coke and retrieving his clipboard and sliding back in the chair.

"We are moving on Foster tomorrow."

Craig sat up straighter, all musings driven from his mind. "What time?"

"4 a.m."

"Do you think he is going to expect you?"

"We hope not. But we are going to assume he is. I've made Miller disappear so Foster doesn't know for sure what happened. I hope he thinks he chickened out. He's got a day off and we hope he's planning on sleeping in."

Craig nodded, thinking hard. "What are you arresting him for?"

"We only have hard evidence on his involvement with the Shroedinger scandal. That's the one where his department stole the guns, drugs, and money they were supposed to turn in. That, and whatever we can get Miller to say about his second attempt on your life. I'm hoping we can convince Foster to talk once we get him in custody. I'm also hoping the Senator doesn't get too spooked. We are going to leak to the press exactly what he is being arrested for so Senator Oberlin knows it has nothing to do with him."

"I bet he won't talk."

Hawk nodded. "That's what I'm afraid of. I wouldn't be arresting him at all if he weren't trying so hard to get rid of you. He's becoming a real liability."

"What are you going to do if he doesn't give up any connection to the Senator?"

"Not sure." Hawk looked down when he said it. Craig hoped he wasn't thinking of doing something that would put him on the same level as Norman. Like torture him. Craig hoped he was well enough to be there when Hawk started questioning, just to keep his old friend in line.

Hawk looked in Craig's eyes, hardness in his face. "Make sure you and Emma don't leave the hospital until I call you and tell you Norman is in custody."

Craig nodded again. He couldn't believe he was going to miss arresting Norman, but he knew he couldn't go. He knew Hawk would do the best job that could be done. His mind turned to leaving with Emma the next day. He was going home, and she was going with him.

Chapter 14

Dark and dangerous, Norman's mood caused people to scatter away from him without even knowing why. He hadn't been to the mall in years, but the only radio shack in this part of the city was here. He kept watching for a tail but he didn't see one. Either those FBI assholes were better than he thought, or he just didn't have a tail. *Bad move guys, it's going to get some of you killed.*

He had left work early, as soon as he had his shopping list finalized. This afternoon he would set it all up, and then he would leave his house for the last time. He hadn't heard from Miller and that meant either Miller had chickened out and fled, or Miller had been arrested. Norman was betting on the second, especially since the volunteer who answered the phone at the hospital now said "There is no information on a Craig Masterson, sir. No record at all." They were getting smart. Plus, Dr. Paloma hadn't returned his calls over the last two days.

If Miller had been arrested, they would be coming for Norman soon. Norman was determined not to be caught with his pants down. He was determined not to be caught at all.

Norman entered the radio shack. The only two employees here were both scrawny, pimply-faced teenagers. Norman hoped they knew their shit. Since they were teenagers, they probably did.

He gave the kid behind the counter his list. "I need all of this and a way to operate it remotely."

The kid raised an eyebrow and opened his mouth like he was about to make a joke, but one look at Norman's face killed that joke in his throat. He walked to the shelves and started pulling off products.

His trunk full of electronics, Norman drove home. He would need to work quickly outside before he lost the light. He started laying wire and drilling holes, setting up and camouflaging cameras and tripods and other, more dangerous things. After 3 hours of work outside he was ready to move inside. He repeated most of the actions inside, but didn't bother with camouflaging. He broke a pane of glass out of his living room window facing the driveway and pointed a bullhorn at the street, a speaker and a semi-automatic rifle behind the bullhorn. At 7 o'clock, satisfied with his work, he grabbed the bags he had packed the night before, changed his clothes, and left the house for good, not bothering to look back.

***

Norman's mood was not even lifted by the thought that he got to play dress up again. His dreams of becoming police chief of Westwood Harbor were gone, shattered and scattered to the four winds. He needed a new dream. A new plan. Even if he couldn't be Norman Foster anymore, he needed to be somebody playing in the big leagues. He needed to be in control of himself and other people. He needed to have a say in how things were run, how people felt. Time to go see the senator.

He was pretty sure he knew where he would find the senator at this hour. He parked behind the large brick building downtown that housed the Senator's home offices. He slipped out of the car and walked around to the front. Normally, when he dressed up he went for roles that required as much confidence and arrogance as his normal life did. But today, as a janitor he wasn't sure how to play it. He didn't pay enough attention to janitors to know what their mood or persona was. Maybe they had a persona that said under-the-radar, don't look at me. Norman tried it out as he was walking around to the front. He rounded his shoulders a bit and tried to look smaller. He wasn't feeling it. *Damnit!* He pulled his gray-green hat over his head low, and tried to shrink into his gray-green coveralls. Maybe he could pull this off better with a tool of the trade. A mop, or a bag of garbage. A prop to help him feel more in character.

At the front of the building he pulled out his keys. The senator probably didn't know Norman could get into this office. There were a lot of things the senator didn't know.

He locked the door behind himself and took the elevator to the fourth floor, most of which was the senator's personal office space. After hours, he didn't need to worry about the building guards, but of course he was on camera. The senator could worry about that detail.

The elevator dinged open. He stepped out and listened. Oh yes, the senator was here alright. Music drifted down the corridor. Norman turned towards the doors, work boots heavy on the polished, glittering tile. He tried the handle of the large double doors at the end of the hall. Locked. That's OK. Norman pulled out his keys again and quietly unlocked them. He swung the door open.

The entryway was empty. He heard the senator mutter something Norman couldn't make out from around the corner of the large, open office. A tinkle of feminine laughter followed. Norman was willing to bet that wasn't the senator's wife. He crossed through the entryway and rounded the corner.

Senator Oberlin looked up immediately. He was fully clothed, while his blond 20-something was totally naked and sitting on his desk. Norman noticed strawberries and champagne. *Celebrating something? Or just being a filthy old man?*

The Senator's eyes narrowed. He drew himself up to his full height. "Who the hell are you and what are you doing here?" he demanded in his most dangerous tone.

"Relax *Frank,*" Norman offered in a conciliatory tone. He took off his hat so the senator could see his face. "We've got some business. Perhaps you should show the lady out."

Senator Oberlin took a step backwards into his chair, but quickly recovered. "Barbie, darling, give us a minute." He gestured to the door behind him. Barbie picked up something lacy and red and scooted out the door.

Oberlin sat down at his desk and moved the food out of the way. He motioned to Norman to sit in the dark, leather chair opposite his desk. Norman sat on the arm of the chair and waited to hear what would come out of the old man's mouth.

"What the hell are you doing here? You know you aren't supposed to come here." Norman grinned and put a shushing finger to his lips. He took an RF detector out of his pocket and swept the room. Clean.

He sat back down on the arm of the leather chair and raised his big, booted foot to the seat. "The FBI is on to me. Our deal is forfeit. We need a new deal."

The senator studied him, eyes narrow, mouth a grim, tight line. "The FBI is on to you for what?"

"Who knows what they know and what they don't. I won't know till they catch me, but I'm not waiting around for that."

"Are you on the run?" the senator asked nonchalantly.

"Not yet."

"What kind of a deal?"

"I want a position somewhere out of the country until this blows over. When you become president, I want a placement somewhere back here - I don't care what you have to do, change my name, change my face, fake me a background, whatever."

The senator nodded quickly, "Yes, I can do that."

Norman studied him, concerned about his lack of argument or request for details. "Look Frank, I know what you are thinking. You are thinking you are going to get me out of the country and then maybe I'll have a little 'accident' and all your troubles with me will be over. Just so you know, it won't be that easy. If I ever die a suspicious death I have systems in place that will leak to the press every single job I've ever done for you."

Heat flooded the senator's heavily-jowled face. "Now look here," he sputtered. "I'm not planning anything of the sort! And what if you have an accident that has nothing to do with me? And who has this information? Our current deal is that you don't share anything with anyone!"

Norman smiled, glad to see a crack in Frank's composure. He shouldn't feel too comfortable. "If you make sure I am well taken care of, no one will ever find out anything."

The senator rubbed his face in a tired gesture. "Look, I can get you a police chief job in Mexico tomorrow, is that the kind of thing you are looking for?"

"Perfect, make it happen. And I'll need a private jet to fly me over the border."

"Done. I have a pilot in Bakersfield who will take you."

"I'll contact you when I am ready Senator, I'll want to be flying within 24 hours as soon as I give the word."

The senator nodded wearily.

Norman got up and walked out. Senator Oberlin stared after him for a long time.

***

Norman needed to know where Emma was and what she was doing before he could plan how to get her. He wouldn't grab her until the FBI made their move first. If he was going down, as many of them as possible were going down with him.

He didn't have any surveillance on her house anymore, but that didn't matter too much. As long as her new *boyfriend* was in the hospital he was pretty sure that's where he would find her too.

He drove to the hospital and parked his car on the street a block away, still dressed in his maintenance coveralls. He entered through an underground service entrance near the laundry and found a janitor's cart in a utility closet. Before heading up the elevator he ducked into a bathroom and added some makeup to his face to make him look older and darker, plus some hair darkener and fake, heavy eyebrows. He also put a special padded suit around his middle to change his body shape. He studied himself. He could pass for a Hispanic male in his 50s. Pretty good. He just couldn't get too close to anyone who knew him.

On the main floor, his first stop was the cafeteria. Only a few tables were occupied and none of them were anyone he knew. He pushed his cart right on by. He was positive Masterson was out of the ICU by now, so he headed to the recovery floor where he almost immediately hit paydirt. Outside of room 417, two hulking bodyguards stood, looking completely alien to a hospital hallway.

Norman positioned himself at the far end and made a show of cleaning and polishing the floor and everything on the walls. He found an empty room and went in to clean it, occasionally peeking down the hallway. He saw nurses and doctors pass. No sign of Emma or anyone he knew.

When he couldn't stay any longer without rousing suspicion he headed down the hallway to the small waiting area. He sat down in one of the chairs, trying to look like he was taking a break. There was not a lot of traffic in and out, but a few nurses gave him dirty looks, especially the second time they saw him. He longed to follow one of them to the back stairs and throw her down them.

When he decided he couldn't sit any longer he headed downstairs. It wasn't late yet, only about 11:15. He'd had the room in sight for over an hour. Maybe it was too late and he was out of luck. Norman decided to head to Emma's house. If she wasn't there, he could enter through the back door and catch a few hours of sleep.

He made one final sweep through the cafeteria, slowly pushing his cart. No Emma.

"Hey, hey you, janitor!" a man yelled behind him. Heart beating fast, he put one hand on the zipper to his coveralls, ready to grab for his gun, and turned around swiftly. It was a volunteer, evidenced by the blue vest. "Hey, we have a spill in the main lobby, we need some help."

Norman nodded, and turned his cart around. He followed the man into the main lobby. A cart of food had been knocked over by a child near the volunteers station. A volunteer and a cafeteria worker had righted the cart and were picking up all the big pieces of food but a large puddle of soda and water grew underneath the cart. Norman rummaged through his cart and found paper towels to lay down. A giggle from the far end of the corridor caught his ear. His radar went up immediately, but the source of the giggle was too far away. Norman worked quickly and had the spill cleaned up in minutes.

The volunteers thanked him, and he was free to go. He pushed his cart slowly towards the far end of the corridor. Strawberry blond hair tumbled over her shoulders. She laughed and gestured. He had found her. He said thanks to whatever brat kid had knocked over that cart and tried to look inconspicuous.

Emma never even looked up as he pushed by. He busied himself emptying trash on the far side of the large couch she was sitting on with another woman, straining to hear what they were saying.

"So Viv, after I take Craig home tomorrow, we have some, uh, stuff to do and then we should come get you! We can all go out to lunch or something if he's feeling OK. Maybe then we can ask him to help us find out our mom's name."

Norman's fingers lost their grip on the

trash can he was holding. It crashed to the ground with a loud clatter. Emma had found her sister! He hurried to lean over and pick up the trash he had spilled, praying they wouldn't look over at him.

The other woman was talking now "... time?"

"I'm not sure. I guess it depends on when they let us out of here."

"Ok, just text me. I'll be ready whenever."

Norman snuck a look at the two women. Emma's sister was lovely, with wide-set eyes and soft brown hair that she tied loosely behind her head. And her skin was clean and glowing. Just like Emma.

The wheels in Norman's head started spinning a new plan.

Chapter 15

Emma woke, feeling joy spilling over from her dreams. What was she so happy about? Oh right, today was the day. The day she took Craig home. The day where there would finally be no cover-ups, lies, or misconceptions between them. Emma hadn't thought about her vision in so many days, but this morning, laying here quietly in the hospital room next to her *boyfriend,* she thought about it a bit. She wondered what would have happened if she had never had that vision and the relationship between her and Craig had just grown naturally. She didn't think it would be as strong. She wondered how she would have reacted to the news that he was an FBI agent if none of that had happened. Would she have been indignant at the lie? Would they have slept together already?

Emma didn't know, but she was sure that's where today was heading. Her body felt like a piano wire, stretched almost to it's breaking point. It had been so long since a man had touched her, strummed her. It had been even longer since a good man had touched her.

She sat up and looked over at Craig. He was sleeping easily, deeply, the rise and fall of his chest apparent from over here. She looked at the clock. 5:30. The excitement had awoken her early. She snuck to the door, wanting to talk to one of their guards, find out about Norman.

Peeking out the door, she saw no guards. The sight seemed so strange and out of place to her. They'd never not had guards.

She stood silently, trying to decide what to do. She tiptoed to Craig's phone and checked it. Nothing. She texted Hawk, "what's going on? No guards."

She needed to use the restroom. Ordinarily she would have gone down the hall so as not to wake Craig but with no guards outside she didn't want to leave him alone. She wished this was a hotel and she could lock and bolt the door.

She lay back on the bed, some of her excitement tempered by the anxiety she now felt. She took some deep breaths, willing Hawk to text her back.

An hour later, he finally did. "I called the guards to me. We needed the bodies. Norman shooting at us in standoff at his house."

Emma flinched. She couldn't believe it. Norman was in a standoff with the FBI? "Please don't let him shoot anyone," she prayed. *Especially Hawk.*

The door whooshed open and a nurse came in for morning checks. She smiled at Emma and set about setting up a tray next to Craig. Craig started waking up. "Good morning Mr. Masterson," she said brightly. The doctor wants your IV out. Without letting Craig even get a word or rub his eyes she took his arm and started unpeeling the tape. Craig winced with pain as his hair pulled out of his arm, but smiled and winked at Emma. His smile wilted as he saw

Emma's wide-eyed look of concern.

When the nurse had the IV out, she gathered up her things and left. Emma shoved the phone into Craig's hands. His face hardened as he read the text. "Hawk will be OK. He's well trained at this kind of stuff."

Emma nodded, trying not to be scared, hoping a good word would come quickly.

The door opened again and Craig's doctor strolled in, hands in pockets, with a large grin on his face. "How are you feeling today Mr. Masterson?"

"Great doc, and I'll feel even better when you let me out of here."

The doctor smiled and started his examination, peering in Craig's eyes, and at his healing wound. "You sir are ready to go. The nurse will be in shortly with your paperwork to sign. Just be certain to do your aftercare, deal?"

"Deal," Craig smiled and shook the doctors hand.

Emma felt her excitement building again. "You really don't have any pain or anything?"

"I do, a little, along the path of the bullet, and everything still feels tight, but I feel like I have most of my strength in that arm, and I don't feel tired anymore. I would say I'm about 85%." Craig stretched his neck to both sides and lifted up his right arm, flexing the muscles. "So where's the clothes Hawk brought me?"

Emma and Craig both washed up while they were waiting for the paperwork. Craig changed out of his hospital gown and into the clothes Hawk had brought for him. When he came out of the bathroom Emma's breath caught in her throat. He looked so strong and big, ducking his head to avoid hitting it on the bathroom door frame.

He smiled and walked to her chair, grasping her hand gently. "I can't wait to get out of here. Did Hawk say we can go yet?"

Emma hadn't thought about this. She texted Hawk "Can we leave?"

"He didn't text me back for an hour the last time."

Craig shifted his weight from side to side, looking like he was itching to go. "Let's get some breakfast at the cafeteria and see if we hear from him by then."

As Emma and Craig walked out of the room hand in hand, Emma started feeling scared. She turned inward, trying to figure out what she was scared of. Craig. His goodness. His rightness. Today felt like the first day of their life together and she suddenly felt herself lacking, inadequate. What she didn't know about Craig she could learn, but she thought about what she did know. She did know he was a good and decent and kind man who seemed to have no issues. No dark secrets. No hidden, horrible past. Hawk, yes, now there was an enigma with secrets, but Craig? He was an open book. A wide open, issue-less book. He probably grew up with a mom and a dad and played little league and had a dog and a white picket fence and the whole 9 yards. He didn't seem to have anything *wrong* with him. And she did. She had so much wrong with her.

Emma tried to push these thoughts aside. It's not like they were getting married, they were just leaving the hospital. But Emma was pretty sure they were going to end up in bed, and this is what was scaring her. After 7 years she felt like a virgin again. She wanted Craig, wanted him badly, but she was also terrified to have him. He was so *good*, and she was so broken.

Alone in the elevator, Craig nuzzled her neck. "Mmmm," he sighed, breathing in her scent.

Emma's senses heightened. Her nerves sent off fireworks that marched up and down her spine with the attention. The man was so big, so right, so hers. *Get a hold of yourself Emma! You've laid yourself bare for this man. He's already seen your worst, your insecurities, your indecisiveness. He's not going to go running when he finds out you like to eat cookies in bed or sometimes you don't brush your teeth in the morning till you've gotten to work.*

She let herself relax a little and curled her hands around his neck, urging his lips up to hers.

Ding. The elevator opening to the crowds on the main floor parted them. Emma's cheeks burned hot as people she didn't know eyed her.

In the cafeteria, Craig piled food on his plate like he hadn't eaten for weeks. Emma tried to keep her breakfast light. She felt a little queasy still. All of a sudden she didn't know if she was nervous for her and Craig or nervous for Hawk, or nervous for Norman? Of course she wasn't nervous for Norman, right? He deserved anything he got. But still she hated to see anyone

151

hurt or suffering. A black sense of foreboding filled her in an instant.

At their table, she checked Craig's phone. Nothing from Hawk. She slid it across to Craig. "Here, it's time you get your phone back."

"Thanks," he smiled around his mouthful of bacon and slid it in his pocket.

Trying to lighten her mood, she teased him a little. "I turned away 4 of your ex-girlfriends so you might want to text them."

His face grew serious. "Emma, I know we haven't talked about this, but there hasn't been anyone for me since Lucy, my fiance. That's been three years almost. What I had with her..." he broke off, eyes shining, voice heavy with emotion.

Emma's heart leaped into her throat. Oh why had she mentioned ex-girlfriends?

Craig continued, "What I had with her spoiled me for casual flings with casual women." He looked down. Emma reached across the table and took his hand. He looked back up and smiled his lopsided smile, making a ghost of a dimple appear on one side. "I guess what I am trying to say is I think you are really special Emma. You remind me a bit of Lucy - but not in a messed up, I'm-so-hung-up-on-my-ex way. Just in your quiet strength and your grace and in how you make me feel. And I'm not just messing around here. I haven't told you this yet Emma, but I love you. I suspected I was falling for you on our second date, which is why you asking out my friend hurt me so bad. I once asked you to move in with me and I am asking you again, will you move in with me?"

Emma leaned forward, lightly licking her lips. Her queasiness was gone; she felt like she was floating. She'd never had a man tell her so clearly and wonderfully what his feelings were. She felt about to burst with joy.

She squeezed his hand. "I love you too. You are the only man for me. I'd love to move in with you when things calm down a bit." Tears fell down her cheeks, unbidden, unnoticed by her. Craig scooted around to the chair right next to her, took her in his arms and kissed each tear away from her cheeks, oblivious to the people eating and socializing around them.

Emma felt her body respond to his touch. She flushed, her fingers twining in his shirt and pulling him closer. She decided right then and there that she would give Craig Masterson everything she had to give. She knocked down those final walls in her brain and gave herself over to him mentally. She was his.

"We should get you home," she whispered throatily, her mouth smooth against the roughness of his cheek.

"Yes, right now" he responded, his voice a low growl in his throat. He pulled his phone out of his pocket and checked it. Nothing from Hawk.

He sat still for a second, indecision on his face. "We can't stay here all day, there's no telling how long the stand off will last. I think we are safe if we go home."

Emma nodded and nibbled lightly on his left earlobe. He groaned. Emma thought she had never heard a sexier noise. "Call us a cab," she whispered in his ear.

Craig pulled out his phone again, suddenly noticing his surroundings, the hard chair he was sitting on, the people around him talking in low voices, a few of them looking at him and Emma. He shifted in his chair. *Yeah, let's get out of here.*

He called a cab, then leaned over and whispered in Emma's ear, "We should head to the lobby. You walk in front of me."

She looked at him quizzically. "Why?"

He pulled her hand into his lap, brushing the hard ridge under the zipper of his jeans.

"Oh!" she gasped, eyebrows high. "Oh," she giggled, a large grin spreading over her face.

She got up, grabbed her bag, and pulled him behind her, walking swiftly. He kept pace. When they had almost reached the end of the tables and the crowd had thinned she stopped abruptly and bent over. "Ooh, a penny!"

Craig didn't expect it. His most tender part ran full speed into her backside. A little thrill of contact bordering on pain ran through him. She almost collapsed on the ground in giggles.

Craig grinned, grabbing her hand as she stood up. He wiped the grin and tried to make his face stern. "You're playing with fire sweetheart, don't make me find a broom closet."

She giggled again, her cheeks glowing red at the thought. He pulled her to the lobby, finding a quiet corner where they could watch for the cab. He pulled her around against the wall and pressed his length against her, trailing her neck with kisses.

She went almost limp against him, sucking in her breath. It had been so long. Her nerves were on fire, begging for more, pleading for harder, more fervent kisses. His lips were slow, careful, like he was afraid he could break her. His hands, resting gently on her waist, twitched and suddenly were moving, roaming, rubbing up and down her jeans, over her hips, gently lifting and squeezing one butt cheek, hooking under her t-shirt and thrilling her bare skin. They were hot, burning her through her jeans, sending heat through her body, and she swore she could feel every flame between her legs. She clung to him, forgetting to breathe, forgetting to move, forgetting this was a two person show. Her head lolled back as her body tried to process the magnitude of sensations.

A honk startled her out of her reverie. She peeked over Craig's shoulder and saw their cab just outside the double doors. "Our cab," she breathed. He didn't stop, didn't slow, just kept rolling his hands across her body and his lips across her skin. She tried again, wanting to get someplace private but never wanting him to stop. "Craig, our cab is here." The cabby honked again. He pulled her to him as close as possible one last time, still incredibly gentle, but hard enough that she could fell his stiff, pulsing length against her belly. Oh she wanted to get her hands on him.

He released her gently with one final, exquisitely gentle kiss to her collarbone, then picked up her bag and his bag, and pulled her to the cab, swiftly, with no thought for who might see how turned on he was.

Chapter 16

The cab ride was short, or it was long, she didn't know. Craig's lips found hers and forced everything but the thought of him and what he was doing to her from her mind. She'd kissed him before, but none of her prior experiences had prepared her for the fiery path his tongue burned inside her mouth when they had no ability to go any farther. Trapped in the back of the cab, she couldn't shed her shirt or take off his jeans, distracting them both from the kisses. His spicy, sweet mouth probed hers, licking her lips open, tasting her like a hummingbird tastes nectar, sucking first her bottom lip, and then her tongue itself until Emma was a warm puddle of desire. The heat radiating up from between her legs felt like enough to set them both on fire. Oh she wanted him, this gentle, sweet, strong man. She wanted to take everything he had to give and give it right back, tenfold.

Craig's kisses, ever gentle up to this point, began to heat up in intensity. He sucked harder, speared into her mouth with more strength, and pulled her to him more urgently. His hands twined in her hair, alternately smoothing it and pulling it, driving her out of her mind with desire. The smell of him, strong, clean man and a touch of aftershave, pulled at her senses, demanded she pay him tribute. "We're almost there," he broke contact long enough to whisper in her ear. The words struck her physically, sending butterflies hurtling through her stomach. This was finally happening. It had been so many years. He was so perfect.

The cab pulled up in front of his large, brick building. He handed the driver several bills and climbed out, running around to help her out the other side. He locked eyes with her, intimately holding her gaze, grabbing their bags and her hand, and walking backwards, pulling her with him. At the door, he swiftly entered the alarm code numbers and put in his key, sweeping her inside in an instant.

Door closed, he pulled her to him in the hallway, his voice a low rumble, "I'm never going to let you go Emma Hill. You are all mine now." Emma shivered at his words and the passion in them. This is what she wanted. She wanted to be owned, consumed, taken. She suddenly felt glad she was a woman, soft and sweet and consumable to this wall of masculine energy before her. The bags forgotten on the floor, Craig snaked his hands around her ass and lifted her off the floor as easily as if she weighed nothing. She twined her legs around his hips and squeezed their bodies together. His mouth sought hers, and she gave it over, willingly. He carried her slowly down the hallway, kissing her like he had in the cab, finally stopping and propping her up against the wall.

His lips never left hers as she heard keys jangle and a door slide open. She twined her hands in his hair, simultaneously thrilled and terrified that the moment was finally here.

He pulled her away from the wall and walked them into the apartment. He left the door standing open and walked straight to their left, putting her gently down on a bed after 10 or so steps. She looked up at him, wanting what he wanted. Wanting to know exactly what he wanted. He kicked off his boots, his eyes never leaving hers. She followed suit, dropping her shoes to the floor. He took his t-shirt over his head and threw it behind him. She sucked in her breath. His chest, so broad and muscled, made her forget where she was for a second. She just wanted to get her hands and tongue on it.

She licked her lips and pulled her own shirt over her head. He smiled down at her gently, his dimples peeking out. She didn't want that gentle smile - the one that said I'll go slow and be careful with you - she wasn't a china doll! She hooked a leg around his thigh and pulled him in, dropping him to the bed on top of her. His white teeth moved in and nipped at her pink, lacy bra. Her sexiest bra that she had specifically asked Jerry to bring to her at the hospital in anticipation of this moment. He pulled the bra back with his teeth, his hot breath goosepimpling her skin. She couldn't stand it anymore and reached behind her ripping the bra off, wanting his bare skin against hers.

His breath sucked in at the sight of her. "You are so perfect," he whispered looking from her face to her breasts and back again. His husky voice turned her on even more. She pawed at his chest, wanting to touch every inch of hot skin.

Her intensity seemed to fuel him. He dropped his mouth to her right nipple and grazed it with his teeth, letting lose a little growl of desire from deep in his chest. His mouth clamped on and he teased her nipple with his tongue, while tracing her other breast with his hand.

Finally! The pleasure washed over her, She wished he had two mouths and four hands. She wanted him to touch every inch of her. Suddenly, the desire to be totally naked was overwhelming. Her mind screamed for his hands in all her most intimate places. Shoving her hands between them she undid her jeans and pressed them down. All that was left was her underwear and she'd be naked, vulnerable, *his for the taking*. Oh she liked the thought of that. She wanted to be taken. Taken with abandon. Taken with passion. She was giving it, now she wanted him to take it. She wanted to tell him, *Take Me*. She wanted to scream it out. She wanted even more to tell him something nastier, dirtier, better, but she could never, in a million years dream of saying that out loud. She worked her mouth a little, trying to get up the courage to say something naughty, something to push him past his controlled gentleness, something to make him rip off her underwear, tear off his own pants, and pound into her with every ounce of force he could muster.

Her mouth opened and closed but nothing came out. She'd been the good girl too long to just shed the image in her own head like she had shed her pants. *Fine. If I can't say it, I'll show it.*

Frantically, she tore at his jeans.

***

Inside Craig's head he was thanking his lucky stars. He pulled back a little, the hard nipple from the perfectly pert and lush breast popping out of his mouth, looking slick from his saliva and oh so inviting. He glanced at Emma's face, her mouth open slightly, her head thrown back, all that strawberry-blond hair jumbled and tousled everywhere and thought he had died and gone to heaven. Emma was shy and sometimes even reserved about things - he wasn't sure what she would be like once he got her alone in his bed. So far, her passionate kisses and frenzied grasping had been pushing him closer and closer to that edge.

He didn't want to go over the edge though. She deserved gentleness, thoughtfulness, caring, love-making. The last thing he wanted was for this to be over in 5 minutes. But oh, it had been so long since he'd had a woman in his bed. Especially a lovely, sweet, *innocent* woman like this. A ripe strawberry, practically begging for him to pluck her, taste her, do what he wanted with her.

She had shed her pants and then dug at his until he pushed them down and kicked them off. Now there was nothing between them but his underwear and her panties. His were standard blue cotton boxers, decidedly unsexy he was sure, but her underwear? Oh they were exquisite. He took one more sucking tug at her nipple and then headed down to check them out on a more personal level.

Her hands twined in his hair, pulling and

pushing. He kissed a trail down her stomach, skimming his fingers over the pink lace. This tiny piece of fabric was all that was between him and *her*. He brushed a thumb over the very center of her and was gratified with a keening from the back of her throat. God he loved that sound. He would give anything to hear it again. Lightly, as lightly as he could, he caressed the spot again, and again through the sheer fabric. Her breath hitched, her fingers convulsed at his scalp, and, oh yes, the light moaning wail came again. "Yes," her heard her whisper.

He dropped his tongue to her sweetest spot and gently probed through the lace. Her heady, sweet taste and scent filled his senses. She moaned again with more intensity this time, dropping her hands to tear at the blankets beneath her.

As much as he hated to see those lacy panties go, he also couldn't wait till they were on the floor next to everything else. He hooked a finger around them and pulled them down, half lifting himself out of the way, intending to go back and finish the job he had started. She stopped him, wrapping her legs around his hips again tightly. His erection was throbbing, demanding, pulsing with each heartbeat, and when she pulled him close, it connected with her now-bare sex. He leaned forward, holding himself up on his hands, looking at her flushed face and pink, inviting lips. Her eyes were closed, her head thrown back. "Craig." The word was spoken as a prayer, a beseeching plea. "Please." She opened her eyes and locked gazes, the heat he saw traveling straight through to his groin. "Now," she whispered. She reached for his waistband and tried to shed his underwear.

He pulled it down and flung it away himself, his engorged flesh free and pressing directly against hers. He groaned a little, his control almost gone. She grabbed his rock hard erection with her surprisingly soft, small hands. His hips bucked at her searing touch. He ground his teeth together against the overwhelming urge to be inside her in one swift movement. She pulled and released and pulled harder, guiding him to her. "Condom," he breathed, reaching into the drawer in the little table by the bed. Within a moment, he had it on and could wait no longer. Back between her legs he dropped his thumb lightly to that tight bundle of nerves, wanting to give her as much pleasure as possible. She gasped and threw her legs around his hips again, urging him into her.

He obliged her, gritting his teeth against the desire to plunge and plunder, slam and slam again. He guided himself in gently, oh so slowly. She felt so good and so tight, pressing against him on all sides. No words could describe the ecstasy of this first meeting, this first entering, this first melding of their bodies. She was still, completely motionless, save for her bird-like hands flying to her mouth, seemingly to hold back a cry. The cry came anyway, a low moan, building in strength the farther in he went. It morphed into a tiny gasp and for a second he saw a flash of pain on her face. He stopped, letting her adjust. Her brow smoothed and she sighed, eyes closed, looking blissful.

He began again, pushing, pushing, oh so slowly, until there was nowhere left to go. He was seated. They were one. He took a breath and told himself "gently, gently," most of him desperately wanting to be anything but gentle. She was so beautiful. A light sheen covered her breasts and stomach. Her lips where he disappeared into her body were the most delicate shade of swollen pink he had ever seen. He could stare at her forever, all that hair flowing everywhere and her soft, feminine body accepting him so fully. He glanced at her face again and her eyes were open, devouring him with their intensity. She whispered something that he couldn't quite make out, but what she wanted was clear by the hard look of desire on her face. Gently he began to take her, make her his. The friction was unbearably sweet. Her breasts called to him and he leaned forward to catch one gently in his teeth.

The desperate keening sound erupted from her throat again. "Yes," she cried, head thrown back, breasts pushing into his face. His sense of control shattered at that, and all he wanted was to be the one to make her say it again and again. Harder he thrust. Her voice urged him on until she seemed to lose the ability to form words. Her body tensed beneath him and her hands flew up to tear, unrestrained at his back and shoulders. His own release threatened to take him, but he held it off until he saw her sated. When she collapsed beneath him, all tension gone, muscles like jelly, he gave one full, final thrust and shuddered over her, into her, finally falling on top of her, spent completely from the most incredible orgasm of his life.

She lay limp beneath him, her breath still tearing in and out of her throat. He kissed her behind her earlobe. "I love you."

She giggled and ran a hand from his buttcheek to his neck, making him shiver. "I loved *that*."

He chuckled, "Oh yeah, but you don't love me anymore?"

"Oh, you're ok." The light teasing in her voice made him love her more. Made him want to see what else she would love.

But reality was quick to reassert itself. In the hallway, he could hear his phone bing-bonging. A text message. Was that the first one or had he just finally noticed it?

Chapter 17

"Oh crud," Emma breathed, trying to sit up. "I wonder if they got Norman?"

"Yeah, me too." Craig pushed to his feet and padded out to the hallway wearing just his socks.

"Don't you have neighbors?" Emma yelled after him.

"They are all FBI, on the scene with Hawk, I am sure."

"Oh," Emma said to herself. This entire building housed nothing but FBI agents? There must be at least 15 apartments, maybe more. She hadn't really gotten a look at Craig's place to see how big it was.

Craig came back in, studying his phone. Emma took a moment to admire his body. She hadn't gotten to see much after he took his underwear off. He was big, of course. Naturally big through the shoulders and chest. That alluring muscle on his side that well-muscled men seem to have jutted out and made her want to jump on him all over again. She avoided looking right at his genital area - she felt shy about that all of a sudden, so she jumped her vision to his legs. She hadn't actually seen his legs yet. They looked tough and masculine too. She sighed inside her head and hugged herself a little. How did she manage to deserve such a hot boyfriend?

She smiled up at his face, but he was frowning.

"Uh, oh, what happened?" she asked, foreboding pushing away some of her afterglow.

"Hawk says for us to stay in the hospital. Says Norman won't give up and has the house boobytrapped so they can't get in."

Emma winced. "Did you tell him we already left?"

"Yeah, I'm texting him back now."

"Do you think we should go back? I promised Viv we would meet her for lunch."

He chewed on the inside of his cheek, cocking one hip like he was perfectly comfortable naked. Emma shivered and pulled her legs up. She wasn't quite as comfortable. She started eying her clothes strewn on the floor.

"Well, the hospital isn't necessarily any safer than any place else. The security guards don't have guns or anything. If somehow Norman got past Hawk and came for us there we actually would have been sitting ducks. I didn't even have a gun."

He crossed the room and placed his hand on a small black box sitting on his dresser. He pressed a few buttons and a door popped open on the front of the box. Two heavy, dangerous-looking guns were inside. He took one, popped out the magazine, pushed it back in, chambered a round, and double-checked the safety. "Now I do."

He put the gun on the dresser, closed his gun safe, and started pulling on his clothes. He smiled at her. "It's too bad we couldn't just hang out here all day."

She smiled back. "Yeah, we barely even got started."

Craig threw back his head and laughed. "You feel like that too huh? I guess it's been a long time for both of us."

He tossed Emma her clothes and she started putting them on.

"So where to?" he asked. "We could get Vivian and head to the hospital for lunch, just to make Hawk happy. The food there isn't too bad."

Emma nodded thoughtfully. "Can we stop at my house? I need some fresh clothes. I wore these yesterday."

"Sure, it's on the way to Vivian's hotel."

***

Driving to her house, Emma's sense of foreboding grew. "Did Hawk say anything else?" she asked Craig.

"Nope." Craig handed her the phone so she could read the text messages herself.

She sent him a message. "What's going on?" but she didn't expect to hear back from him very quickly. She opened her mouth to tell Craig how she felt but closed it again, not wanting to sound silly.

Craig broke the silence. "I can't stop wondering how it's going at Norman's. I hope he hasn't shot anyone."

Emma sighed, relief slipping over her. So he felt it too. "Yeah, me too."

Craig pulled into her driveway and stopped the big truck. She eyed the house. She hadn't been here in 4, 5 days? It felt like forever. The house looked different, smaller, closed in on itself. She shook her head, trying to clear it.

"I'll just be a second," she said, jumping out of the truck. Behind her, she heard Craig turn off the engine and get out, then felt his presence behind her on the doorstep.

She unlocked the door and ran left, down the hall to the bedroom, pulling clean underwear, jeans, and a mint green babydoll out of her dresser and closet, suddenly wanting to be out of here quickly. She shed what she had on, throwing everything in the hamper, and changed quickly. A swift stop in the bathroom to run a comb through her hair and maybe grab a tube of mascara and she was ready. Emma stopped short. Had she just heard a thump from the living room? She shoved the mascara in the pocket of her jeans and headed out of the bathroom, nerves suddenly on high alert.

Tip-toeing down the hallway she instantly knew that coming to her house was one of the worst decisions she'd ever made in her life, right up there with marrying Norman. She wanted to call for Craig, but didn't dare call for him at the same time. From her vantage point she could see about a third of the living room. Nothing was moving. The front door was closed. As she reached the end of the hall she peeked around it and saw Norman, bent over Craig, who was motionless on the ground. Norman shoved his gun cruelly into the back of Craig's skull with one hand and patted him down with the other. Finding Craig's gun in the boot holster he pulled it out and crammed it into his own waistband.

He stood, pulled a dark tube from his back pocket and began screwing it onto his gun. Emma's mind went blank from terror. He was going to shoot Craig! Again! "No!" she screamed, running for him. Norman backed up, pointing the gun at her now. She threw her body on top of Craig's, two fingers going reflexively to his carotid artery. His pulse was there, strong and fine. "Craig, wake up, Craig, are you ok?" Her voice shook with desperation. How could this be happening? How could Norman be here? Had he gotten away? Where was Hawk?

Norman barked out a short, hateful laugh. "Give it up Emma. He's dead. He just doesn't know it yet. And neither do you apparently."

He finished screwing the suppressor onto the gun and pointed it at them both. "Get up now Emma, don't make me shoot him through you."

Emma curled her body around Craig's head and chest. "Go ahead Norman," she demanded, her voice low and dangerous.

Norman remained silent. Emma waited him out. She wasn't moving. Her mind raced. Maybe if she stalled long enough Hawk would show up.

"Why Norman, why do you want to shoot him so bad? Just leave him alone!" Isn't this what you were supposed to do with crazy gunmen? Keep them talking?

Norman barked that horrible laugh again. "He would shoot me if he had a chance cupcake, don't you think he wouldn't."

Cupcake. That's what Norman had called her after they were married. She never had liked it, and she was pretty sure he knew it. But what in the world made him think he could call her that now? Oh yeah, he pretty much did whatever he wanted, up to and including murdering innocent people apparently. What did he care if he called an ex a name she didn't like?

"No he wouldn't Norman, he would never shoot you, even though you would deserve it!"

"What's he been filling your ears with cupcake? Stories about me? I figured as much. And you wonder why he has to die. I'm giving you one last warning Emma. I will shoot you. I can shoot you somewhere that won't kill you but you will gladly move off of him just to avoid being shot again, and then he'll be shot anyway, so why bother getting yourself shot too? How about your right arm there, you won't need it where you're going."

Emma's mind spun. Where I'm going? Won't need it? What was going on here?

"Where am I going Norman? Why are you here?" She asked quickly, pulling her arms in underneath her body, suddenly struck with how horribly exposed her legs were.

"You're going with me."

Emma saw a chance. A slim chance of survival for Craig. She had to take it. She dropped her tone, trying to find conciliatory.

"Norman, what if I get up right now and go with you willingly, will you leave him? Can you just leave him and not shoot him? I swear I won't give you any trouble if you just leave him here on the floor. Don't hurt him."

"Sweet on him Emma? Don't want your new boyfriend to die?" Norman's tone was blank, not the sneering she would have expected. The blank tone terrified her. She was deathly afraid a bullet was following it.

Emma thought back, racked her brain. Was there anything that had given her an advantage over Norman when they were married? He had hated her tears. That wouldn't help her. Sexuality maybe, but that probably wouldn't help her right now. Maybe later. If there was a later. What to do now? Lie? Tell the truth? Say nothing?

She heard a soft metal against metal sound behind her. Norman cocking the gun to let her know her time was truly over. Her hands raised automatically to her head as she waited for the blast.

"Norman listen to me," the words spilled out of her mouth quickly, her brain not knowing which would come next. "Norman, really, what do you want from me? What can I do for you? Anything. I'll do anything." The last thing she wanted was to beg Norman, but she would if she thought it would help. Anything to keep him from putting another bullet into Craig's head.

His silence stretched out, filling the room.

"Norman, I'm going with you. You want me with you. We can go, right now, together. I'll go with you totally willingly if you just leave him be. Just let him lay here on the floor and we can leave right now. I swear I won't fight you, I won't run, I won't yell, I won't struggle. I'll be yours."

A heavy clink on the floor next to her. She peeked out. A pair of handcuffs. "Cuff him," Norman ordered.

She huffed out the breath she'd been holding in relief. Eager to comply, praying Norman truly meant it, she rushed to put the handcuffs on Craig, pulling his heavy arms backwards behind him. From this vantage point, she thought she could see what Norman had done. Craig's wound on the right side of his neck near where his skull meets it had looked so good, almost totally healed this morning. Now it was puffy and weeping again. The whole area looked purple and swollen. Emma imagined she could see the tennis ball-sized lump growing as she watched. Hot tears burned her eyes. The bastard had hit Craig in the head, right on top of his injury. Probably had pistol-whipped him. Emma could only imagine the repercussions of two horrible injuries in the same exact spot in the space of less than a week. No wonder Craig was still unconscious. And she had wanted to come here. Her hands shook, banging the handcuffs together. *Please God, if you are watching, please help Craig be OK. And please send Hawk over here soon.*

"Now go sit on the couch. Pull your legs up onto the couch and cross them."

She did, her heart beating so loudly in her throat she could barely hear.

Norman bent over Craig, pulling the handcuffs, testing her work. He went through Craig's pockets again, finding his car keys and his phone. They both went in Norman's pocket. He backed up, still facing her, and backed right into the kitchen, taking his eyes off of her for a second. She sat, staring straight ahead. What could she do? If she ran or screamed or grabbed the phone he would shoot Craig. So she sat.

He opened a drawer and reappeared, an electronic tablet like an iPad in one hand, his gun in the other. He put the tablet down on the table, watching it and tapping it's screen intently. After a few minutes he looked back at Emma, his eyes unreadable.

He looked around the room. Emma watched him with terror in his eyes. What was he looking for now? Whatever he was looking for, he didn't seem to find it.

"Get up," he demanded gruffly. She scrambled to her feet.

"I'm putting my gun away. You are going to walk a foot ahead of me. If you run, scream, shout, or otherwise try to attract the attention of anyone, I will turn around and put a bullet in lover boy's brain in an instant. And if you get in front of me again, I'll put a bullet in your's too. Understand?"

"Yes," she said, with all the strength she could muster. Who knew where this was leading to. She was going to need to be strong.

Chapter 18

Craig came to slowly, his head a splitting mass of agony, his vision doubled, his right arm refusing to answer his commands. What in the hell had happened?

He had been walking slowly through Emma's house, waiting for her to grab some clothes so they could go get Vivian. Something about the house felt off, different, anxiety provoking. He was just about to pull his gun and go investigate the rest of the house when a blinding pain exploded in his head and he knew no more.

He lifted his head and looked around. His head threatened to crack. He put it back down, closed his eyes, and listened. Nothing. He was alone in this house. Emma was gone. Norman was gone. He knew it was Norman. Who else would it be? Ahh, he was such a fool! There was some other asshole in Norman's house shooting at his team while Norman slipped over here and took Emma.

Craig gritted his teeth against the pain that was about to come and pushed himself forward until he could force himself into a kneeling position. That was actually a little better. He blinked his eyes, trying to clear them. The room swam. His hands were manacled behind his back. *Why wasn't he dead* was the real question.

Emma must have done something. God he prayed she wasn't hurt. He prayed he could find her. He couldn't lose another woman to that monster Norman. His vision darkened immediately when he thought of what Norman had done to Lucy and what Norman could possibly do to Emma. If he lost Emma too ... he wrenched his mind away. He couldn't go there. That dark pit of despair was full of jagged spears that could rip him to shreds in a second and leave him writhing in his own mental agony on this floor, a threat to no one. A savior to no one. What he needed right now was to move, to get out of these cuffs, to get Hawk and go after Norman.

Get out of these cuffs. Quickly. He had never tried before himself, but he knew it could be done. He'd had criminals escape cuffs on him a few times. He struggled to his feet, breathing against the dizziness that threatened to overcome him. He bent forward at the waist and scooted his handcuffed hands behind his back, down the length of his legs. He was too bulky for this, it worked better for thin guys, but it had to work. There was no way he could get the cuffs over his head like some of the double-jointed women could.

His hands were stuck at his butt. He pulled out harder with his arms and pushed down and backwards with his shoulders. Oh shit! An epithet exploded in his head as he started to tip, falling forwards onto the floor on his face.

He lay there for a second, trying to clear his head. The pain in the back of his neck was now monstrous, all consuming. Nausea threatened him. He didn't have time for this!

He pushed himself to his feet again, compartmentalizing the pain, and walked over to a wall to brace himself. If he couldn't get it this time he'd need to go try to find a neighbor and hope they believed his story and would help him.

Pressing his shoulder against the wall he leaned forward again, dragging his hands down his back and pushing-pulling past the swell of his butt. He got it! The rest was easy. He pulled his hands down to his feet and stepped backwards through them. His handcuffed hands were in front of him.

The phone! He ran and grabbed the handset and awkwardly dialed Hawk's number. It went straight to voicemail.

"Hawk! That can't be Norman inside the house! Norman came here and took Emma. Hawk he's got Emma, we have to go after her." His voice broke on the last word.

He hit the button and tried another call to Dennis. Nothing again. He left a message to have Hawk call him at this number right away, it was an emergency. He tried every man in their team, and none of them answered their phones. Of course he wasn't surprised, but he was terrified. He hung up the phone and started looking for a shim or a bobbypin to get him out of these cuffs.

A thought struck him. How long had he been unconscious? What if they'd just walked out the door? He ran to the front picture window. No one was on the street in front. He grabbed a jacket from the nail on the wall, covering his handcuffed wrists with it and ran outside, searching both ways for any sign of them. Nothing. No cars, no people.

Ok, back inside, get these cuffs off, and think! Craig ran into the bathroom and rummaged around until he found a bobby pin. He bent it carefully until he could fit it inside the keyhole of the cuffs and pop them open. First one, then the other. Free!

Still no phone calls. He checked his pockets. No keys, no phone. He couldn't just sit here and wait for the damn phone to ring! He was heading to Norman's house. He made up his mind, he was going to hotwire his own truck. He could be there in 10 minutes. Racing back out the door, he heard the phone ring. He ran back in, a glimmer of hope lighting up his chest, and picked it up. "Hawk?"

"Go," Hawk growled, gunshots ringing in the background.

"Hawk, Norman isn't in that house. Can't be. He came and took Emma. Emma's gone! He knocked me out and kidnapped Emma." Craig felt about to break down, about to lose it.

Hawk was silent. Craig could hear his mental wheels clicking and turning though. He waited.

"Where are you?" Hawk's voice betrayed nothing. But Craig knew he was feeling the same desperation Craig was. Norman was getting the best of them again. And another woman might pay for it with her life.

"I'm at Emma's house. We left the hospital. We came here to get her clothes. He was waiting here for us. I didn't see him, but I know it was him."

"How long ago?"

Craig's eyes searched the small living room for a clock. "Um, we got here around 11, I think and it's ... 11:40 now. My best guess is I was out for 15 minutes. I've been awake for 5. So he probably took her 15 or 20 minutes ago." Craig's heart broke with this news. 20 minutes? Norman could be anywhere by now.

"What is he driving, do you know?"

"No, no idea."

"His car is here in front of the house, so he's in something different. We're about to do a hail mary swarm on the house. I'll leave Carruthers to mop up whatever shitstorm we find in there and come get you. I'll be there in 10."

The phone went dead in his ear. 10 minutes. What in the hell was Craig going to do for 10 minutes? Search for clues, that's what.

He started in the kitchen, where he was pretty sure Norman had been holed up, waiting for them. Nothing caught his eye, except a partially open drawer. Nothing out of the ordinary in there. The lock on the sliding back door had been jimmied, he could see that from here. So that's how Norman got in. He stepped onto the back porch and found a pile of cigarette butts. Emma didn't smoke. Norman normally didn't either, as far as he knew. Uncertainty tugged at him. Maybe this hadn't been Norman after all? His right hand snuck to the back of his head, gently probing the large, angry lump there.

If it wasn't Norman, then how did he know to hit me in almost the exact same spot where I was shot? Maybe it wasn't Norman who shot him either? No, it was! He knew it was.

Heading back into the house he checked Emma's bedroom for anything out of the ordinary. Nothing back here. Seeing her nicely made bed and neatly hung clothes in her closet made Craig's heart hurt faster. He had to *do something*! He checked the alarm clock on the dresser. 10 minutes had passed. He ran back out to the front of the house to look for Hawk.

***

Hawk barely slowed down long enough for Craig to jump in the big, black, government-issue Ford F350 he was driving. "Where we headed?" Craig asked.

"HQ, gonna see if Norman owns any other vehicles and check street cams."

Fucking genius! Craig craned his head to see if there were any cams in this neighborhood. He didn't see any right here, but that didn't mean there weren't any. Craig took three deep breaths and crammed on his seatbelt. Hawk had the temporary bubble lights and siren blaring, moving as fast as possible.

Dodging cars and streetlights, Hawk's attention was firmly on the road, but he'd been doing this long enough to be able to talk too. "How's your head?"

"Hurts like hell," Craig admitted.

"We should get you back to the doctor. 15 minutes is a long time to be unconscious."

"Find Emma and you can take me

anywhere you want. But until we find her ..." he trailed off, knowing he didn't need to explain himself to Hawk. Partially to change the subject, but mostly because he really wanted to know what SOB was working with Norman he asked, "So who was in the house?"

Hawk grunted. "No one. He had it rigged up to a computer that he was operating remotely. The bastard was shooting at us and talking to us, and watching and listening to us from somewhere else. Emma's house maybe."

Craig felt like he had been punched in the gut. Norman was one smart, slippery, son of a bitch. What if they couldn't find him before... before the *unthinkable?*

They pulled in front of the large brick building and ran in straight to the batcave. "Call Carruthers, see if he found anything we can use pertaining to any other vehicles or homes Foster may own." Craig nodded.

Hawk slid into the chair in front of the rows of monitors, flying his fingers over the keyboard. Craig knew if there was anything to be found, Hawk would find it.

Chapter 19

Emma didn't dare yell, scream for help, or even drag her feet. It was obvious Norman meant business. Until they were far enough away that she knew he wouldn't turn around to put a bullet in Craig's brain, she planned on doing exactly what he wanted. But after that, all bets were off. She had never hated anyone in her life, but her blood boiled and her brain fried at the thought of Norman's audacity and cruelty.

He led her six blocks away on foot to a giant RV he had parked in the empty parking lot of the community playground. It was modern, big and blocky, with brown sidewalls and dark, tinted windows. He unlocked the side back door and pushed her inside. Immediately her eyes started devouring the room, looking for her future means of escape. She noticed an apparent modification that didn't make any sense to her. A large metal ring screwed into the middle of the floor.

"Sit down," he told her, shoving her towards the ring, causing her to stumble.

She recovered and went to the couch.

"Not there," he growled. "On the floor."

Her eyes on him warily, she got down on the floor.

"Hold your hands out."

He produced two more sets of handcuffs from a drawer and handcuffed her wrists in front of her, then her handcuffs to the large metal ring. She was secured well. Her heart sunk. Sitting this way she couldn't reach anything with her hands.

He left her there and went up two stairs and opened a door in the very back of the RV. She craned her neck but couldn't see anything in the room but a corner of a bed. He closed the door behind him and was gone for about a minute. She heard his muffled voice say something, and then he was back out, smiling. *What the hell? Was there someone in that room?*

"Now Emma, I'm so glad you've decided to come with me. We have got to get out of here very quickly before your boyfriend wakes up and raises the alarm, so excuse me." He turned and walked up to the driver's seat and prepared to drive away.

Decided to come with you? Are you insane? Yes, she was afraid that Norman probably was insane. Maybe always had been. Fear niggling at her heart and brain threatened to turn to full-bore terror. What if she couldn't get away from him? What was he planning to do with her? What if Craig was dying on the floor in her living room? What if he didn't wake up and no one found him there for a day or more? How far away would she and Norman be? He was fleeing of course, she knew that. There was no life for him in Westood Harbor anymore. He could be at the Mexico border in about 9 hours. Is that where he was headed? Of course he'd have to cross somewhere but if he managed to get her across the border would even Craig or

Hawk be able to save her? They could disappear so easily in that country.

She couldn't let that happen. She had to get free the next time they stopped. She had to do whatever it took to get him to unhook her from this metal ring.

The big rig rumbled to life and shook and swayed as Norman started driving them to where ever they were going. Mexico, she just knew it. Her heart sank every time she thought of it. Alone, in an RV with Norman in another country. A country that didn't always cooperate with the United States. A country that the FBI couldn't operate and investigate freely in like they did here. Her thoughts spiraled out of control. Was he going to kill her? Rape her? Sell her? Make her pose as his wife? Terror coursed through her body. She started to shake, the handcuffs clinking together horribly.

Get a hold of yourself Emma! Don't hand yourself over to him on a silver platter! You can get out of this! You can't sit around and wait for Craig to rescue you. The thought made her realize again that Craig needed rescuing himself right now. Tears threatened to burn at her eyes. No! No crying! Right now you have to come up with a plan! You don't have one second to spare on crying.

She took a few deep breaths, hoping to calm herself, and glanced around. Her back already felt uncomfortable on the floor so she decided to lay down, stretching out with her hands over her head. She heard Norman begin to whistle from the driver's seat. *He really is a psychopath.*

She was in the living area of the RV, with her feet stretching towards the driver's seat. The sink and oven with multiple cabinets above and below were on her right. The fridge and couch and table were on her left. She didn't see anything that would help her get out of here. There was a large window next to the table, and a few small ones on the other side. She wondered if she could break the large one. She didn't see anything heavy enough to break it with. Norman's gear had to be in these cabinets thought. She bet he had several guns and other weapons somewhere. If only she could get loose! Of course if she got loose he would be on her in a second, way quicker than she could figure out where his gun was probably.

The RV picked up speed. Emma tried to figure out where they might be. There was a freeway entrance about 5 miles from her house that would eventually lead them to I-5. She wondered if they were on it yet. She couldn't see anything out the windows but sky and clouds.

Her mind turned to a plan. She needed a plan. What did Norman want from her? If he wanted sex, that might be her way out of this. But could she really use sex as a way to get out of this? Did she have a choice? What would be better, trying to seduce him and then possibly finding a way to use it to her advantage and get free? Or being raped? Either way she was going to be screwed by him if that's what he wanted. Her mind tried to imagine kissing him and making him think that she wanted to. Her stomach turned at the thought.

She closed her eyes and hid her face under her right arm that was stretched over her head. Come on Emma, if this is your only chance you have to do it. You can't overpower him. You don't have a single weapon. You can kiss him with passion if it's the only way.

But she didn't think she could.

***

Something was changing. The RV was slowing down. They were pulling to the right. Were they stopping? Emma jerked out of the almost-sleep like state she had been in for what felt like several hours and sat up. Her shoulders ached from being stretched out for so long. She scrambled as close as she could to the metal ring and faced the driver's compartment. Norman stopped the RV and turned it off, pocketing the keys as he stood up.

He looked at Emma and smiled. The smile looked flat and evil to Emma, and totally fake.

"You may think you want to scream or try to escape Emma, but I wouldn't do that if I were you. Sure, I can't shoot Craig anymore, but your sister is still here."

Emma felt like screaming. *Sister? He knew about Vivian? He had Vivian here?* Suddenly she felt cold, colder than she'd ever felt in her life. Her vision threatened to blacken. She clenched her teeth together hard enough to crack them and leaned forward, trying to keep from passing out. *Sister. He had Vivian.*

Norman laughed a little laugh and went on. "She's quite lovely you know, just as lovely as you Emma. And clean too. That perfect combination." He walked past Emma and sat down on the couch. "I'd love to hear the story of how you two finally found each other."

Emma didn't say anything. She just concentrated on breathing. Breath in, breath out.

"You don't want to talk right now? No matter. We'll have plenty of time later." His voice grew hard. "Unlock yourself, now." He threw the handcuff keys into her lap.

She looked up. Unlock myself? He was pointing his gun at her. The one with the silencer. The expression on his face made it clear he meant business. He would shoot her in a second if she tried anything.

Heart hammering in her chest she grabbed the keys and unlocked both handcuffs, dropping the keys to the floor and rubbing her wrists.

"Pick up both sets of handcuffs and stand up."

She picked up the handcuffs and the keys too, palming them, wondering if she'd get a chance to keep them.

"Turn around and head into that room back there." He motioned to the door in the back of the RV.

She climbed the two steps and opened the door. Nothing. The bed was empty. There was no one in here. She couldn't believe it! He'd been bluffing! He didn't have her sister! She turned around, not sure what she meant to do, her face set in hostility. She wanted to kill him. She wanted to shoot him with his own damn gun.

Too bad he still had it trained on her, his finger on the trigger.

His lips pulled back in a smile more evil than the first. "Don't get any bright ideas Emma, she's here. Turn back around."

She did. Norman did something behind her, a whine of hydraulics filled the room, and the bed started lifting from the ground, tilting onto one side. Beneath it was an open, hollowed out space. Vivian lay in this space, hands over her head, handcuffed to another metal ring. Her eyes were closed. She didn't look to be breathing.

"Vivian!" Emma rushed to her and her fingers went right to Vivian's pulse point. Her heart was beating, fast and thready. Like she was terrified. But her face was relaxed as in sleep or unconsciousness.

"You bastard!" Emma whirled around, hands balled into fists. "What did you do to her? How could you do this Norman? You are supposed to be one of the good guys! You are supposed to be a cop!"

"Yeah, well your boyfriend and his friends took that life from me, didn't they?" he sneered.

"What? What? You can't kill people and expect the FBI not to come after you!"

His voice dropped low and deadly, conniving. "Who have I killed Emma?"

Emma eyed him, not sure what he was looking for. Did he want to know how much she knew? How much Craig knew? She whirled back around to Vivian and checked her pulse again. "She's sick Norman. Get me an aid bag."

"She's not sick. She's fine. She's just

having a nice trip."

Emma's mind reeled. A nice trip? Her eyes flew to Vivian's arms. A spot of dried blood stained the left one on the inside of her elbow. "Oh my God. What did you inject her with Norman?"

"Don't you worry Emma, you'll find out soon enough." His voice changed again, to the hardened, I-mean-business tone. "Lay down next to her, handcuff yourself to the metal ring."

Emma's mind raced. Was this the time to try something, anything? She couldn't try to seduce him. She could barely keep herself from spitting in his face. Maybe just keep him talking.

"Why Norman, what are you going to do with us? Where are we going?" She searched his face.

Very deliberately, he swung his gun from her to Vivian. "Now Emma."

There was nothing she could do, except what he wanted. She lay down and handcuffed herself as loosely as she dared.

He came forward and tightened the handcuffs until they hurt. Then he opened the drawer next to the bed and pulled out a syringe. Her eyes grew wide when she saw it. "No Norman, don't. I'll do anything you want. I won't scream. I won't try to escape." She couldn't tear her eyes from the syringe. She'd never done drugs in her life.

Norman put one leg over the piece of wood sticking up that the bed would rest on when it was back in place. He put a rubber tourniquet on Emma's arm, obviously planning to inject her.

Emma felt her mind shattering, trying to fly away. Her breaths tore in and out of her throat, blocking any further speech. She kicked her legs a little and Norman looked at her, death in his eyes. With his left hand he pressed his gun directly against Vivian's temple.

Emma stilled immediately. She squeezed her eyes shut and waited. She wondered if she'd ever wake up from this, and if she did, where would they be?

She felt the prick of the needle.

Chapter 20

Nothing. Of course not. Craig tore his eyes from the last house they had surveillance on that Norman had ties with and glanced up at the clock. An hour had passed since they arrived and they still weren't any closer to finding Emma. They didn't even have anything to go on.

"Damnit Hawk! I can't sit here for one more second! I gotta go do *something*. I'm going to go walk Emma's neighborhood and start asking the neighbors questions."

"Dennis is already there. He has only found two people who are home and neither of them saw anything. He just texted me."

The cordless phone on the counter rang, startling Craig, who jumped up to grab it. "Masterson," he said into the receiver.

"Hey Craig, one of the cops who used to work with Norman called me and gave me some information that might help you." It was Carruthers. Up until this morning he had been undercover in the police department.

"Yeah, what?" Craig could taste his excitement. He grabbed a pen and paper.

"He says that he's known Norman was dirty for years now and he's been keeping a file on him, trying to get people to listen. He said he has to be careful of who he told because the first time he tried to go to Norman's boss he almost got fired. Anyway, he went back through his file and found 3 vehicles that Norman or his team confiscated on search warrants but the vehicles never actually showed up in the yard. A brown, 2007 Winnebago Adventurer, a red, 2010 Honda Civic, and a black 2002 Maserati Gran Turismo."

Craig scribbled the vehicle names on his paper. "What is a Winnebago Adventurer?"

"I think it's a big motorhome, you know, like a RV."

Lights bloomed in Craig's mind. They were looking for an RV. "You got license plates?"

"No, no license plates. The best he could do was the names on the search warrants."

Craig's excitement waned a little. That probably wasn't going to help them, but at least it was something to check out. "You tell that cop thanks from me. What's his name? I'm going to want to thank him personally someday."

"Huff. Jared Huff."

"Got it, thanks!" Craig hung up the phone. "Hawk we got a little break. I bet you 100 bucks we're looking for a big brown RV. Have we seen anything like that yet on any of the street cams?"

Hawk looked up, interested. "Nope, nothing, what you got?"

Craig explained the situation. Hawk lapsed into silence, his thick, dark eyebrows screwed together tight.

Craig paced behind the row of monitors, thinking hard. They could put out a roadblock. No, if Norman was leaving town he'd be long gone already. They could notify the state cops, put out an APB on a brown RV and see what came back. Risky though, state cops might push Norman over the edge. It would be better if he and Hawk could get a visual on the vehicle somewhere and go get it themselves. He kept pacing, his options getting smaller and smaller. He peeked at Hawk, whose fingers were dancing over the keyboard again.

Hawk was the computer master. He didn't need Craig's help. There had to be *something* else he could do. He couldn't just sit here.

"I'm going to the police station, I'm going to start asking questions."

"The Chief will throw you out when he finds you. He was livid when I didn't notify him this morning that we were going in hot on Norman. I still haven't decided if he would have tipped him off or not."

"Let him throw me out! Maybe I'll find something first. Maybe a look at this file Huff was keeping would help us." Craig headed for the door. He stopped short. "Wait, give me your phone. Norman took mine."

Hawk's head tore away from the computer screen to stare at Craig, his eyes wide. "Norman has your phone," he breathed in excitement.

His whipped back around and his fingers tore at the keyboard.

Craig ran to him. "What, what? Can you trace my phone?"

"Yep, it's got a tracker in it. All your phones do," Hawk said, referring to the other agents on the team.

Craig watched Hawk's fingers fly over the keyboard, hope finally blooming full in his chest.

Come on, come on, find it. His hand reached out and grabbed the truck keys off the counter. As soon as he had the slightest inkling of a location he was gone. Hawk could catch up later.

Craig watched a map come up on the screen. Hawk groaned and Craig's heart sunk. "I've only got a last known location. That means he smashed the phone I bet."

"Well where is it?"

"A playground 6 blocks from Emma's house on Centurion Street."

"Do we have any Cams on the playground?"

Hawk thought for a second. "Good thinking. I doubt it but I'm checking now." Two more maps popped up on the closest monitor. Then some street view pictures. "Nope, but just let me try something."

The constant click-clacking of the keyboard with no results was enough to drive Craig batty, but he gritted his teeth against the irritation. They had to find *something*. They *had* to catch a break.

Now Hawk was looking at google street view of the area, all the way around the playground. "Found one," he muttered under his breath.

"Found what, found what?"

"Just hold on, gotta concentrate here," Hawk told him. He had a screen pulled up that was nothing but text flying across the screen. "Yes," he breathed and switched back to a browser view.

"See this gym across the street? The

Better Body. I hacked into their security cameras. There's a good chance they can see the parking lot. If they can't, I'll try the flower shop next door."

Craig could see grainy, black and white camera images being rolled backwards in time. "I just gotta go back an hour and a half..." Hawk sucked in his breath. Craig craned his neck to look. A huge, brown RV was rolling out of the parking lot.

"Oh my God, go back farther," Craig urged him.

"There, that's Emma! And Norman!" We got him! We need the license plate on that RV!"

"Working on it," Hawk's voice was low and tight and his fingers flew. The RV moved forwards and backwards until he got a perfect head-on view. He zoomed in on the license plate but it was too grainy to read. "Just gotta optimize it ..."

"I'll be right back, I need to get loaded up," Craig said, jogging out the door. He came back within 5 minutes, wearing tan khakis and a dark blue polo shirt, a sub-compact G27 Glock in his boot and a Glock 23 on his belt.

"Anything?" he shot at Hawk.

"Yeah, we got the plate number. I just loaded it into the automatic license plate reader system for all the bridges on every highway within a 30 mile radius. We should get something back any second here."

The screen flashed. I5, bridge number 483. Craig held his breath. Hawk entered some numbers on a calculator. "102 miles out, headed south."

Craig's desperation threatened to overtake him. "If he's headed to Mexico we'll never catch him before he crosses the border."

Chapter 21

Swirling, down and dark, Emma was pinned in a hot tub, somehow her foot was stuck in the drain and she was being pulled under, drowning, dying. She couldn't breathe. She felt desperate for air. She was alone, and no one would care when she died. She had nobody. No wait. She had Craig, and Jerry, and she had Vivian. These people would care when she died. Her breathing came a little easier. Vivian, she had family now. She had a sister.

Emma opened her eyes, her tongue thick in her mouth. She wanted to breathe hard and suck in great gasps of air, but her lungs wouldn't respond. The room above her pressed in on every side, dark, so dark, except for a pinprick of light to one side.

"Em, I'm here, can you hear me?" a whisper came from the dark.

Vivian's voice! The room slammed into place, but it wasn't a room at all. They were in the compartment under the bed in RV, which swayed and rumbled beneath them.

Emma opened her mouth and purposely drew in as much oxygen as possible, still feeling like she was suffocating.

"Shhhhh, it's ok, it's the drug he gave you. It's going to make you feel like that for a few more minutes until it clears."

Emma tried to relax. She couldn't, she still felt like she was drowning.

"It's called Lofentanil, it's like Heroin, but 100 times more potent and it lasts for 2 days. He already pulled over and came back to check your breathing once, so I figured it was safe to wake you up."

"Wake me up? How?" Emma whispered back sputtering, trying not to gag on her own tongue.

"He has Narcan too, in case of an overdose. I gave you the Narcan." Emma knew what Narcan was. They carried it on the ambulance. If someone overdosed on an opioid like heroin or morphine, most likely it would depress their breathing to the point where they might stop. An injection of Narcan would kill their high and get them breathing again within a few minutes.

"How, h-how," Emma tried to ask something, but her mind lost it.

"How did I get the Narcan? I've been working on getting out of my handcuffs since he first brought me in here and I finally did. My hair tie has a long metal piece on it and I used that. I knew how to do it because we got some handcuffs stuck on my friend Theresa at a bachelorette party last year. Then I was able to break out that board at the top and get out into the room. The Narcan was in the same drawer as the other drugs. He's got a ton in there."

Emma rolled her eyes towards Vivian, her hands still handcuffed and her muscles as heavy as lead.

"So that's your ex-husband huh, nice guy. If you don't mind though, let's not invite him over for Christmas this year."

Emma couldn't believe her ears. Was that a joke? Norman had kidnapped both of them and had God-knows-what plans for them and Vivian was joking about it? A short giggle shot out of her in spite of herself, but it quickly dissolved into tears.

"Shhh, shhhh, Emma I'm sorry, I didn't meant to joke."

Emma pulled herself together, and dragged in more deep breaths. "No, I'm sorry. You're right. Norman shouldn't come for Christmas this year." Emma tried to smile but only grimaced. "Did he give you the drug too?" she asked her sister.

"Yep." Emma could barely make out in the dim light that Vivian was smiling.

"Then how come you aren't unconscious? Were you faking earlier?"

"Yes, I was faking. Remember my tumor? Well I take a medicine every day that competes with opioids like Lofentanil for receptors in the body, so they don't affect me. When he injected me I wasn't sure what he expected to happen but I thought pretending to pass out was a safe guess. When you passed out and your breathing was so slow I figured it must be an opioid. I was so happy to find the Narcan, although Norman seemed to think you were breathing fast enough."

"Maybe I need some more Narcan, I still feel really out of it."

"I don't think so, it just needs another minute or so to work fully. But you will need more in an hour or two maybe. I'm not sure how long Narcan lasts, but Lofantanil can last for 2 days."

"2 days!"

"Crazy, I know. We could be deep in the heart of Mexico by then."

"Do you think he's taking us to Mexico?" Emma whispered frantically?

"Oh yeah, after he injected me he said 'I sure hope you can speak Spanish,' and laughed."

"Oh man, we gotta get out of this bus. If he gets across the border with us, who knows what he'll do with us! And Craig will have a harder time getting to us in Mexico too, I bet." Emma tried hard to think. "Can you get these handcuffs off of me?"

"Yeah, but maybe we should have a plan first. If the RV stopped right now, I would put mine back on and pretend to be passed out," Vivian motioned to her handcuffs above their heads, still fastened to the metal ring.

"Where is the empty syringe?"

"I ripped a little hole in the carpet next to the board and shoved it in there."

"Good thinking." Emma was a little in awe of her sister's ingenuity. And very glad for it. If they were going to get out of this mess, they would need all the good ideas they could come up with. As much as Emma would like to imagine that Craig was hot on their heels and about to swoop in and save them, she knew the reality was probably very different. She took a moment to hope that he was OK, where ever he was, and then she turned her mind back to their problem.

"Ok, how about the window at the back of the RV, just over the bed. Can we get out it? We could wait until Norman had to slow down or stop for something and then jump out and just run."

Vivian thought for a second. "Maybe. I didn't look closely at it. Should I go look, or should I get you out of the handcuffs first?"

"You should get me out of the handcuffs. Just in case." Emma was starting to feel a bit better. Her muscles felt lighter, like maybe she could stand and lift things.

Vivian fished a hand into her pocket and came out with a heavy duty purple hair tie with a small metal clip holding it together. Or at least it had been a hair tie. Vivian had pulled it apart so now it was just a piece of fabric with the clip at one end. She stuck the metal clip in the keyhole of Emma's handcuffs and levered it up just a bit. After a few tries, she was able to pull first one cuff off, and then the other.

"Ok, I'm going to go look at the window, stay here." Vivian low-crawled to the top of the compartment, near the metal rings and pushed the board she had broken fully out of the way, then levered herself out, pushing with her feet on the metal rings.

Emma watched her go, then brought her arms down to her sides and massaged them, her ears alert for any sign that the RV was slowing.

After a minute, Vivian crawled back in,

feet first, and wiggled down to lay next to Emma again. The excitement on her face gave Emma hope.

"It's an emergency exit. There's a big red handle to pull and the whole window pops off. That's our plan. He's going to have to stop and get gas soon. We pop that window off and run. We'll have to be quick though, because only one of us can fit through it at a time."

"Ok, that's the plan then, let's get out of here."

Vivian crawled out first and Emma followed. Her legs didn't want to support her at first, they felt weak and rubbery. But boy did it feel good to stand up! Sunlight streamed through the windows. It was hard to believe they had just been handcuffed to the floor under a bed by a madman.

Emma stretched a little and bounced up and down on the balls of her feet, trying to get some circulation going. She eyed the window. It was very small. She put one knee on the bed and read the instructions on how to get it open, and then tried to see how far the drop was on the other side. She thought maybe she saw a ladder that they could climb down but it was hard to tell from this angle.

Vivian reached past her and pulled the little dresser drawer open. Inside was a red drawer organizer, with over 20 syringes inside.

Emma's eyes grew wide. She lifted a few syringes to read the labels. Lofantanil, Heroin, Narcan, Oxycontin. What was Norman doing with all of these? Remembering what Vivian said, she slipped a couple of Narcan syringes into her left pocket. As an afterthought, she grabbed a handful of Lofantanil and slipped them into her other pocket.

Emma looked around the room for anything else they could use. The door was closed tightly, so there was no way Norman could know they were up, as long as they didn't make too much noise. She got up on the bed and opened the cabinets above it. They were full of Norman's clothes. She started pulling clothes out and feeling through them, looking for anything that could be a weapon. If she knew Norman, he probably had a full cache of guns and knives hidden somewhere.

Finding nothing, she moved on to the small closet on the side of the bed. More clothes, shoes, boots, empty holsters. Emma checked every holster and felt every piece of clothing. She even got down on her hands and knees and looked for secret compartments in the floor of the closet, but came up empty. *If only Norman had stored a gun back here. She was pretty sure she could shoot him if she had to.*

She cast her mind back to the open area behind the driver's compartment. Would Norman store his guns in one of the cabinets up there? Likely the big one next to the fridge? Or was there a secret compartment somewhere else in the big vehicle.

She looked out the window. Dry, flat land flew past. One car was behind them far off in the distance. Occasionally a car passed them going the other way. Were they on I-5? This stretch of road didn't look very heavily traveled. If they were on I-5 they must already be south of all of the big cities.

She craned her neck, trying to see a street sign or something that would give her a clue as to where they were. Vivian got up on the bed next to her and whispered "I'm just going to get into position here. As soon as we pull over or start slowing way down I'm going to pop this window."

"Ok." Emma kept watching out the window. For miles and miles it seemed like she saw nothing but flat, dry, empty land. The signs on her side passed too quickly for her to see what they said, and the signs on the other side were too far away on the divided highway. She felt sleepy and dull, the swaying and constant noise of the RV lulling her into a relaxed state. She tried to fight it but found herself wanting to lay down and curl up on the bed...

Vivian pinched her arm, hard. Emma sat straight up, alarmed. They were slowing down! She jumped up and crammed her face against the side window, trying to look in both directions at once. No sign of civilization, just miles and miles of empty, dry land like before. Were they coming up on a gas station?

The RV took an exit ramp, turning onto a side road, then an immediate hard right onto a dirt road. Dust flew everywhere, partially obscuring Emma's view. No gas station this way for sure. Norman kept slowing. Oh no! If he just pulls off onto the side of this road and comes back here there will be nowhere to hide! No cover, no people, no nothing. It was at least 3/4s of a mile back to the freeway where there would hopefully be cars zooming by. He could pick them off easily if that's what he decided to do. He probably could even catch one of them and pull her back here. But what could they do? They didn't have time to get back under the bed. They had to go for it. He couldn't catch them both. Emma was determined to give her sister a fighting chance at getting out of this mess.

"Do it, open it!" she hissed to Vivian. Vivian pulled the red metal bar, putting all of her weight into it. It gave, and the window popped right off, falling onto the bed. Vivian stuck her head out and looked around.

She pulled back in. "We can climb down the ladder, it's on the far side but we can reach it." she whispered to Emma. The RV was slow enough now that there wasn't any road noise to mask their voices.

"Go, go." Emma made shooing gestures with her hands. Vivian turned around and stuck her feet out the window first, holding on to Emma to steady herself.

The RV came to a full stop.

She felt for the ladder with her foot, finding it and reaching a hand out to grab the ladder with. Emma flipped her feet around and poked them out the window. She could hear Norman's footsteps in the RV. Frantically, she felt around with her right foot for the ladder. She couldn't find it. Screw it, she didn't have time for this. She pushed with all her might, trying to heave her body backwards out the window as the door opened. Norman's placid face erupted, eyes going wide as he saw her almost all the way out.

Emma wiggled her hips and pushed harder, raking her shirt up and bruising her breasts on the window. But she got it, her head was out, she was falling to the ground. Ooooph, the air was knocked out of her lungs as her legs collapsed beneath her. A sharp pain shot through her left ankle. Puffs of dust exploded around her. Vivian was there immediately, helping her up. They ran around to the side of the RV where Norman couldn't see them. Emma didn't see anything to run towards except the highway. "Vivian, the road, we have to run to the road." She could hear Norman pushing his way out of the window after them.

They ran. Emma ignored the pain in her ankle as long as she could, but it did slow her down. Vivian pulled her. "Come on Emma, hurry"

"Go Vivian, go, get help. Flag down a car. Tell them to call the cops, go. I can't run any faster. You have to go or he's going to catch both of us."

"No, Emma, I -"

Emma interrupted her, terror in her voice. "Vivian GO, you have to run! You have to tell Craig where we are!" She gave her sister a little push, still running herself.

Emma saw the regret already in Vivian's eyes, but she did as Emma wanted. She turned to the road, tucked her head and arms in and ran. Emma couldn't have kept up with her at that speed even without a hurt ankle. Heck, Norman probably didn't even have a chance of catching her. She was *fast*.

Emma ran too, landing on her hurt ankle as lightly as she could. She could hear Norman behind her, gaining on her. *Well at least he didn't stand at the RV and mow them down with bullets. At least Vivian still had a chance.*

Emma felt a hand entwine in her hair and jerk her to the ground. Norman landed on top of her, driving all the air out of her lungs for the second time in a few minutes. She felt more pain in her ankle, but it was no longer as important as the crushing pain in her ribs.

"Bitch," Norman spat out, trying to catch his breath. Emma squirmed beneath him but couldn't dislodge his hold on her.

Hurry Vivian, please get help, she thought as she writhed in pain in the parched, baked dirt.

Chapter 22

Craig sat in the back of the helicopter, scanning the roads for the large dark RV.

"Hawk, they must have turned off, they had to have, or we'd be on them by now." His voice sounded tinny and strange to himself inside the headset.

"Yeah, I think you're right. If we don't come on them by the next bridge we will backtrack and check Highway 99."

They were less than two hour's drive from the Mexico border. The team on the ground was coordinating with border patrol to stop all RVs and arrest Norman on sight, but Craig was afraid Norman had other plans. They all knew there were plenty of places to cross illegally. Or what if something went wrong. What if he were changing vehicles right now. The bridge cams hadn't picked him up for an hour, and the state police hadn't found him yet either, even though they had the urgent APB.

If Norman slipped through to Mexico their chances of finding him would instantly drop in half or maybe less. Especially if he already had a support team over there. Or Heaven forbid if he had a contact at the border who would just wave him through and claim not to have gotten the message.

Craig's mind ran down a list of a hundred things that could go wrong, a hundred ways that

Emma could be stolen out of his life forever. He squeezed his fingers to the back of his neck, trying to calm the pounding in his skull.

The pilot broke through his thoughts. "Call on the radio for you Agent Masterson, I'm patching it through."

Craig sat up straighter, the road temporarily forgotten. "This is Agent Masterson,"

"This is officer Thompson of the State Police. We've got units headed out to Piers Road just outside of Bakersfield to meet with a woman who claims she was kidnapped. The vehicle description she gave matches your APB."

Craig felt the helicopter bank a hard left and looked up at Hawk. He was listening intently, but gave Craig a thumbs up and a nod.

"Is she OK Officer?"

"We don't know yet sir, we haven't gotten to her. Apparently she flagged down a motorist and he called it in. Officers are 5 minutes out."

Craig looked at Hawk, a question on his face. Hawk held up 4 fingers.

"Ok Officer, tell your guys we are going to beat them there. We are coming in hot. Anywhere to land around the area?"

"Oh ayuh, take your pick. It's nothing but a big, dusty landing pad.

"Thank you Officer."

Craig heard the radio switch off. His heart beat in his throat. Normally he would take a few minutes to calm himself, but he didn't know if it would work today. Not till he found Emma and knew she was OK.

His eyes scanned the ground again, looking for any sign of that RV.

Chapter 23

Norman struggled to his feet, still panting hard, sucking in lungfuls of dirt and coughing them out again. He tried pulling Emma back to the RV by her hair but his grip kept slipping. He leaned down, digging his fingers into her armpit cruelly, intending to stand her up and make her walk.

Emma relaxed her body, trying to make herself dead weight. He stood up and aimed a boot at her ribs. "Bitch, get up, now!" He punctuated the 'now' with a kick and Emma scrambled to her feet, doubled over in pain. She couldn't take another kick. He grabbed her under her left arm and dragged her back towards the RV, moving fast.

Emma coughed and sputtered, tasting blood in her mouth. She felt along her right side with her fingers, wondering if her ribs were broken. Anger blazed in her eyes. She was *not* going back to that RV with Norman. Something in her pocket grazed her hand. *Oh yeah.* She pulled the syringes from her pocket and uncapped them all with one motion, jabbing all of them into Norman's neck with every ounce of strength she had left.

He tried to scream, but sounded strangled.

He dropped her arm and bent over,

tearing the syringes out of his neck one at a time.

As he bent, his white, button down shirt flapped up and Emma saw a gun in a holster. She darted in, unsnapped the holster and pulled the gun out quickly, backing up and thumbing off the safety with it pointed straight at Norman's back.

She kept backing up, slowly, back the way they had came. Her world narrowed to the sight of his back over the gun's sights and the feel of her finger on the cold, hard metal of the trigger. He would fall, or he wouldn't. He would rush her, or he wouldn't. He would retreat, or he wouldn't. She was ready, playing her reaction to each scenario over in her mind. Dust whipped around her, unnoticed.

He pulled the last syringe out and clasped a hand to his throat. She could see tiny droplets of blood between his fingers, slowly dripping to his collar. He turned on her, his face deadly. She saw clearly that he planned to kill her now.

She stopped and planted her feet in the sideways shooter's stance that Norman himself had taught her all those year ago. *Make your body as small a target as possible,* he'd told her. She'd always loved shooting, even in the army. She'd always been good at it too. Her mind didn't want to shoot a real flesh and blood person, but her body didn't care. Her body was in charge.

"Stop Norman, or I'll shoot you." Her voice rang over the desert, clear and strong.

He kept coming, his lip curled up in a sneering, skeptical smile. He was only 5 feet away. She took her aim from his chest, out to his shoulder, held her breath, and squeezed.

The shot hit him in the arm and knocked him to the ground. He screamed this time, a guttural, aching sound. She moved the gun sights back in to land on his chest, still not wanting to kill him though. She healed people, she didn't kill them.

He reached for his boot, probably for an ankle holster. "Stop Norman!" she screamed. His fingers pulled up his pant leg.

She fired again, twice this time, tears streaming down her face.

Norman's body jerked and twisted and he fell to the ground without another sound.

She stood there. Waiting for him to move again. She stood there, as the dust kicked up around her and the helicopter landed 50 feet away. She waited and watched, barely breathing, watching for the slightest movement.

She was still standing, rigid, unmoving when Craig came up behind her.

"Emma, it's me, you can put the gun down."

She couldn't though. He could move at any second. He was just playing possum, she knew it.

Craig put an arm gently around her shoulder, and his other hand over the gun she was holding. "Baby, let go of it, it's Craig, I'm here and you are OK. You did it. He can't hurt you again."

Craig?

She let go of the gun. Her knees gave out and she dropped to the harsh desert ground.

Chapter 24

Emma's fingers clawed at her throat, the taste of desert dust clogging her mouth.

"Shhhh, sweetheart, it's a bad dream, that's all, you're home in bed. Norman is paralyzed in the prison hospital, remember? He can't hurt you. You don't have to shoot him again."

Her eyes flew open. She was home, in her new home she shared with her boyfriend, sleeping in bed. She tried to force herself to relax and take a few deep breaths.

He put his hand on her forehead and smoothed her hair away from her head. "Was that a bad one? Are you OK?"

"Not too bad." She grabbed his hand and held it, snuggling into his bare chest.

He held her close. "Was it the end again?"

"Yeah, the shooting. I keep shooting him over and over again. But this is the first time in a week, so it's getting better." She gave him a weak smile.

"Yep, way better. Dr. Anderson said this would happen. If she's right, then you shouldn't have them at all in a month or so."

She already felt sleepy again, but didn't want to stop talking to Craig. She glanced at the clock. It was 6:40. She didn't have to be up for an hour. Sunlight streamed in the windows, chasing all that was left of the dream away. Vivian was following the moving truck in today and Emma was supposed to meet her at her new place at 10. Emma snuggled into the blankets, suddenly blissful at the thought of Vivian living in Westwood Harbor, only a few short blocks from her and Craig's new place. She almost felt disappointed that work had cleared her to come back so quick after learning the true nature of her 'arrest'. She'd only have a few days to help Vivian unpack before she had to return. Oh well, she did miss her job and she missed seeing Jerry every day too.

No sense getting too happy though. The question of Craig staying or not staying always loomed large in her mind. If Craig had to go somewhere else for the FBI it would kill her.

She looked up at Craig and kissed his chest, and with her lips still pressed up against him she said "yeah, but if you have to leave town, then what? I don't want to try to face the dreams without you here."

"Oh, didn't I tell you?" he said, sitting up a little. "Me and Hawk have been permanently reassigned. We are now working out of the Westwood Harbor FBI office for good."

She smiled against his chest. "How wonderful." She thought for a second. "But what happens when you finally catch that Senator? I know you guys will eventually."

"Emma, I don't care if it takes 6 years, or 6 days. When we finally put him behind bars I am retiring from the FBI forever."

"Really, you mean it?" She jumped up and

kneeled over him. "Don't joke about that Craig, I couldn't take it if you were joking."

"I mean it. Didn't I tell you I always wanted to be a firefighter for real?"

Emma beamed. She couldn't imagine. Craig. Hers, here forever. Did that mean ...? She thought back to the first time she ever talked to him, when the flash of a baby with big dimples and strawberry blond hair had come to her mind.

She twined her fingers in his and brought his hand to her lips. That was tomorrow. For right now, having him here in her bed was enough to keep her warm and happy for a good long time.

The End
<<<<>>>>

Keep reading for a sneak peek into Edge of the Heat 3

Get The Newest Books

Get Early notification of all my new releases and the new release **sales** by signing up for my mailing list at http://www.lisaladew.com

Could You Help Me Out?

I truly hope you enjoyed this book.

Would you please do me a favor and write me a review? **There is nothing more important to authors than reviews.** Let me know what you think of it.

Stay Connected

I love my readers. Yours insights into my books often floor me. Connect with me on
Facebook:
https://www.facebook.com/LisaLadewAuthor
Twitter:
https://twitter.com/LisaLadewAuthor

About the Author

I live in Idaho. I have been married for 18 years to the only man on this planet who will put up with me (I'm a handful) and we have two amazing boys (10 years old and 1 year old at the time of this writing). We have a 7 year old husky/golden retriever mix (dog) who is just awesome and gorgeous. I love computers and the internet. I love my facebook friends. I love books and I love my google nexus. I only buy ebooks these days - they are SO convenient! I like to walk for exercise as much as possible, which hasn't been often since the baby was born. Hmmmm, what else do you want to know? :)

I always, always, always wanted to write when I was a little girl. Stephen King was my favorite author. I stopped being able to read him when my first son was born though (too many kids getting hurt). These days you can probably find me reading Julie Ann Walker or H.M. Ward instead. I published my first book at 41 years old. I'm not sure how it took me so long to do what I really wanted to do since I was a kid. I love writing and I love interacting with my readers.

Dedication/Acknowledgements

This book is dedicated to my husband who is my rock, our sons who are my heart and motivation, and my friends, two of whom I will mention by name here.

Joan Adams, my constant cheerleader. Thank you for boosting my spirits every week with your love for the story.

Lisa Howard, you are like a good editor and agent all rolled into one. Your thoughtful critique and good ideas really have helped me put on my professional author's hat. I will forever be grateful.

And I would like to thank Amanda Harris for creating another cover as hot as the first. Find her here: http://www.stunningbookcovers.com/

Edge of the Heat 3 Sneak Peek

Vivian ran as fast as she could, legs pumping, closing the distance between herself and the road in record time. In all her years of high school track, she'd never run this fast. But she'd never been chased by a madman before. Never been responsible for whether her sister lived or died before. She listened for the gunshots behind her. Knowing if they came, she would again be sisterless. She pushed herself harder, the dust from the cracked ground tearing at her throat. It didn't matter. Nothing would matter if her sister died because Vivian was too slow. Norman was crazy. He'd kidnapped them both, drugged them, and hidden them under a bed in his RV, planning to somehow get them across the Mexican border and then who knows what he had planned. That made him the worst kind of crazy in Vivian's mind.

The road! She'd made it. She almost overshot right into traffic, but managed to stop and start waving her arms at the nearest car. It didn't stop. She kept waving and ran in the road. Cars swerved around her. She got so close to one car that its side mirror hit her left forearm. The pain shook her.

Vivian dragged her eyes open, forcing

herself to wake up before the gunshots came. Again she'd had the nightmare. That made 4 times so far this week. She rubbed her eyes. Sunlight streamed in the window. At least she'd made it to morning this time. Maybe she should go to Emma's doctor. She hadn't told anyone about the dreams yet, hoping they'd go away, or at least lessen. Norman kidnapping her and her sister had been the most traumatic experience of her life. Of course it was going to bother her. But it had been almost a month and the dreams were coming more frequently. Almost every night now.

Her left arm throbbed. She looked at it. A large bruise was forming on the forearm right where the car had hit her in the dream. She must have hit it on the side table. Briefly, she thought about moving the table away from the bed, but then thought better of it. She knew she flailed about during the dreams. What if instead of hitting her arm she threw herself right off the bed? Maybe she should try to sleep more in the middle of the bed, and pile up some pillows around her.

Unbidden, the events after she had reached the road in real life came to her mind. She couldn't seem to let them go.

In reality, the first car she had waved at had stopped. The woman inside let her use a cell phone. She called 911, not knowing what police station her call would go to.

She'd been winded from the run, and it took her a few minutes to get the story out to the dispatcher. The dispatcher put an officer on the line almost immediately and he said he was in touch with Agents Masterson and Kinkaid who were in a helicopter a few minutes out from her location. Vivian wept with relief, almost collapsing on the side of the road. But she hadn't seen or heard a helicopter yet. She looked back over the field and what she saw chilled her. Emma and Norman were fighting. They were close together, but far enough away from her that she couldn't tell who was who or what was happening. She took a few steps in their direction, thinking she had to go back and try to help Emma. But she couldn't. Her legs wouldn't take her. They were rubbery, jelly-like. She felt like a newborn fawn trying to stand for the first time. She sat down in the dust, fear for her sister eating her alive, and prayed. Prayed that Craig and Hawk would get there in time.

The whup-whup-whup noise of a helicopter made it to her ears. *Please let them make it in time.* She saw it, flying closer to the ground than she'd ever seen one before, coming in over the overpass to her left.

And then she heard a gunshot. Then two more. Purest terror shot through her. "NOOOOOOO!" she screamed. In that instant, she knew her sister was dead. Knew she never should have left her sister to die in the desert with a madman. Knew it was all her fault for running. For giving Emma the Narcan that had woken her up under that bed, for picking the lock on their handcuffs and getting them out of there in the first place. If she hadn't done that, Emma would still be alive. They'd still be in danger, yes, but still alive. There would still be a chance.

Vivian pushed herself to her useless legs and tried to run to Emma, tears streaming down her face. Her legs wouldn't go. So she crawled, the hot desert ground burning her hands. She crawled half the distance back to Emma and Norman, sweat and tears and dust doubling and tripling her vision, her own pulse beating in her ears loud enough to drown out any sound.

A shadow fell on her. She stopped and looked up. She couldn't tell who it was, just that it was a man. If it was Norman, so be it. She would accept her fate. But not before she spit in his face.

A silky, masculine voice reached her ears. "Vivian, are you hurt?" Hawk's voice, soothing her as he knelt beside her.

"Emma, where is Emma? Is she shot?" she wailed, not knowing if she was hurt or not.

Hawk had leaned down and taken her in his arms, picking her up effortlessly.

"No, Norman is shot. Emma shot Norman."

Emma shot Norman? Emma was OK? Vivian's brain couldn't quite grasp this. She'd been so sure that her sister was dead.

Hawk carried Vivian the rest of the 1/2 mile or so to get back to the helicopter. Vivian had taken comfort in his hard-muscled chest under her head. His warm male scent of clean sweat and musky cologne had filled her nose. Hawk wouldn't lie to her. She knew it. Emma must really be OK.

Vivian saw Norman on the ground, the desert dust mixing with his blood, turning it orange. Police officers swarmed around him.

Hawk carried her to the helicopter where he lifted her in gently. Emma was sitting there, Craig pressing something against her side. Emma looked at her and burst into tears, pushing herself over to reach Vivian. They had hugged and cried for what seemed like hours.

An ambulance took them both to the local hospital. Emma was x-rayed and treated for badly bruised ribs, and Vivian was treated for 2nd degree burns to her hands from crawling across the hot desert. She never even noticed the pain until Hawk had pointed out the blisters on her hands.

Vivian shook away the mental image of that horrible day and looked down at her hands. It had been almost a month since that day and her hands were almost fully healed. She no longer had to bandage them at all. She remembered Hawk grasping her hands gently and holding a cold compress to them in the back of the ambulance.

Ugh, Hawk. He'd been so sweet after the *incident,* taking care of her, talking softly to her, basically being a nice guy. Then she'd gone home for a few days to get her house in order there and when she'd returned, he was back to his old ways of grunting and disappearing when she was around. He hadn't been downright mean in the last month, whenever they'd seen each other, so that was an improvement, but the sweet, kind, caring Hawk she'd seen in the desert was gone.

Every time she thought of him her heart hurt. She knew she was falling for him. Vivian laughed a disgusted laugh to herself and rolled over in bed, burying her face in her pillow. Scratch that. She'd already fallen for him, head over heels, hook line and sinker - pick your cliché, she was living it. He was just so ... manly. When he walked by, all the women turned their heads to look at him. She'd seen it. He was the epitome of tall, dark, and handsome, and don't forget broad through the shoulders and chest with a slim waist that tapered perfectly above an amazing butt. All she wanted to do was put her hands all over him every time she saw him. Or heard him. His voice was low and gruff usually when she was around. It sent shivers down her spine every time.

Vivian got up and padded to the bathroom, silently berating herself for her superficial lust after Hawk Kinkaid. She barely knew the man. She didn't know if he was smart or stupid, funny or dull, generous or stingy. Well, she did know he was brave. And she knew he was good at his job. And she knew he was the best friend of her sister's boyfriend.

Oh, and she knew that Hawk didn't like her. That much was obvious. Not only did he obviously not like her in *that* way, but he also seemed to think she was some kind of a jerk or something. She didn't know why. She'd never done anything to him. In fact, he'd seemed to dislike her the first time he set eyes on her. She hadn't even had a *chance* to irritate him. Unless it was her looks that had done it.

Vivian sighed and turned on the shower. These circular thoughts about Hawk that never led her anywhere but frustrated were as common as her nightmare.

Yep, definitely time to see a shrink.

CPSIA information can be obtained
at www.ICGtesting.com
Printed in the USA
BVOW06s1802160417
481407BV00005B/61/P